Joshua:
Life After Theos

Patricia Miller

This book is dedicated to my brother, Michael, who taught me the importance of hard work and dedication balanced with creativity and laughter. I will never forget his belief in me and the wisdom he shared in just the short 19 years I had with him.

Many thanks to my family and friends who supported me throughout the writing of this book. With special thanks to Eric Shapiro for his encouragement and creative input.

PART ONE

We become products of our environment.
Sometimes we choose it. Sometimes it chooses us.

1

AVOIDING

Why are Female Earthlings so illogical?
I peered out the second story library window, which overlooked the parking lot. So many women came and went, exhibiting their lack of reason:

High heels even though they hurt, dresses even in the cold...and forget about even *trying* to make them happy.

So why did I waste so much time watching her? I supposed my eyes were overruling my brain. This had happened once before that I could recall:

I was seven, in atmospheric science camp, my gaze forever fused to that one girl whose name I wouldn't go on to remember. Even with my computerized atoms spilling out all over the place, I could not set my eyes on anyone – or anything – else.

Though I winced at the embarrassing memory, my wincing couldn't peel my stare from Emma. Her gold hair, interwoven with the rays of the sun, bounced up and down off her shoulders as she made her way across the blacktop. It was Tuesday, my (secret) favorite day of the week – our day to work together at the university library.

Emma quickened her pace, oblivious to my watching, her own eyes fixed on the double glass doors in the distance. The day was sizzling; most Earthlings were tucked away inside their dwellings, breathing in artificial, controlled air. My spoiled, pampered body liked that feeling, too, but good luck getting me to admit *that* out loud.

She rose a hand, sliding her long bangs to one side, then disappeared through the front doors. I scrambled through the stacks, trying to make it back to my cart before the elevator door dinged, heralding her presence.

Be cool, dude. Just a guy shelving books, that's all.

My cell phone made a *swoosh* sound: a new email. When I looked, however, I got distracted by the date atop the screen: June 16.

Wow. Has it really been that long? Twelve months, two weeks since Mani and I had landed on Earth…and almost immediately went our separate ways. I missed her, but things were better this way. See, Mani, my ex, craves fun – nothing but it, in fact. I'm sure her high school gives her everything she needs. As for me, I belong with adults, just like back on Theos. And I came here to be the first Theosian on Earth, not to waste time on foolish things like video games, partying, and completing homework assignments.

There it was: the ding. Positioning myself behind the stacks, I squinted between the books in her direction. Emma stepped off the elevator and slowed her pace, allowing herself enough time to smooth down that thick, golden hair.

Yeah, she touched her hair a lot. And I had no objection to it whatsoever.

8

Now, whereas secretly gawking at her was fine, her seeing me look at her…well that was a different story. As usual, when her eyes flashed my way, I looked down, evaluating my appearance and straightening my shirt, when a horrible thought entered my mind: *Oh crap. I forgot to wear a dark-colored shirt today. My glowing back will show through this white tee. And my hoodie – it's in my locker!* I had to get it on before someone saw, and by "someone" I of course only mean Emma. I slid between rows of books, easing in the direction of the locker room. I had just about made it when something large smashed into me—the head librarian. *Yuck, did our bodies just touch?*

"Oh, Mrs. Marshall."

"Joshua." Her eyebrows were hovering like a pair of bushy clouds.

"Sorry I ran—"

"Joshua, where *is* your name tag?"

I looked down at my shirt. "Right." I reached into my pants pocket and pulled it out to show her, immediately pricking my finger on its clip. "Ouch."

"Don't let me catch you without it again." She glared at me in that way she always glared at one of her employees when they needed to be put back in line (as if anyone was at all intimidated by *that*).

I haphazardly pinned it to my shirt, knowing I had to get to the locker room, and fast. But to complete my mission meant sliding behind the circulation desk and past the employee break room, too. OK, OK…one step at a time…

Phew. I slid my black hoodie over my head and stepped back out the door. Turning, I saw Emma through the door's rectangular window, heaving her books onto the counter, then sighing heavily and looking at Kaylee, her BFF, who sat nearby, working on a computer.

Upon taking a slightly closer peek, I noticed Kaylee and Emma exchanging glances. Since I was still refining my ability to interpret human facial expressions, I...yeah, I had NO CLUE how to decipher them.

Emma let her purse slip off her shoulder, took a deep breath, and stepped in my direction. I dove backwards, out of sight – I hoped! *Crap, she must have seen me slithering away...*

***

In the break room, my friend Cole sipped coffee while sharing (once again) his predictions about the fate of the Cleveland Brown's coach...

"New year, new coach, right?"

"Yep, guess so." Now, I could certainly hang in these types of discussions, thanks to sports channels and morning radio talk shows, but that didn't mean I enjoyed it. The Theosian sports back home involved far more physically challenging skills than those found on Earth. After all, our bones were way stronger than human bones – nearly unbreakable, in fact. Boxing and bull-fighting, now those sports earned something of a reasonable comparison, but not quite.

Cole had wrestled in high school, hence his bulky, top-heavy structure. The day we both showed up for job interviews at the university, I remembered thinking he was probably just some dumb weight-lifter carrying around the remains of a few too many cheeseburgers along with his ten-word vocabulary. But the moment he introduced himself, I knew better. Turned out he knew a few more than ten. We both worked in the library now: me in the stacks and he in maintenance. Friends ever since that day.

As for my social skills beyond small talk, especially with the females...well, that was quite a different thing. In truth, I didn't plan to get into a relationship – a romantic one, that is. Even though I didn't plan on returning home, a relationship between a Theosian and a Human would be quite taboo on my planet, which made the mere thought of it difficult for me.

My obsession with Emma notwithstanding...

Cole sat at the table stuffing a cupcake into his mouth, biceps threatening to tear his shirtsleeves. He didn't seem to notice me leaning against the counter opposite the door, clinging to my hope the candy machine shielded me from her view. If not, I guess it didn't matter, as I planned to ignore her. Key word: *planned*. But there are plans, and there's reality. The break room door opened.

"Hey, Emma." Cole licked chocolate frosting from his fingertips.

"Hello," she managed in return, her voice cracking. Cole had once told me the cracking voice thing means

11

a girl's into you. *Why does the air suddenly feel too thick to breathe in? Talk about awkward.* I managed a glance at her, for maybe a second, maybe less. *Crap. Did I smile? I did, yeah, just a little, but it was the real thing: a smile. Yeah, that's the way you ignore someone.* I turned away from her. *Yeah. That's the answer. Man, it's a good thing I had this dark hoodie standing by in my locker.*

She walked past me, opened the refrigerator, slid her lunch onto a rack, shut the fridge door, and started for the exit door. I was both thrilled and devastated to see her go.

"Hey, you have a nice day." This was Cole's sorry attempt to make up for my sorrier behavior.

She hesitated at the door. "Thanks," she told Cole. "You too, Josh."

"Yep, see ya around," I whispered, my throat twisting into a knot, as the door closed behind her.

Cole's brow furrowed above his squinted eyes. No chance he was about to return to his tired sports babble. His pinched expression told me without question that I was in for it.

"What?" I asked, fully aware of that question's utter stupidity. He continued staring. I sighed and looked away, then back again, slightly alarmed at the lack of change in his expression, as though he were frozen in time. "Cole, we've been over this before."

"I just don't get you, Josh."

"Cole, it's like I've said—she's a nice girl and all, but…"

Cole interrupted, "But what? I mean, come on Josh—look at her." Cole nodded at me, then looked toward the glass window in the break room door.

Yep, I did it again.

I looked.

She stood at a cart, beside a stack of books, hair shining like golden silk. Her weight shifted to one side, right leg bent, swaying back and forth. I noticed the perfect curve of her legs underneath her jeans. The body of a dancer, for sure. She was shorter than me, about to my nose in height. It never mattered what she wore. She'd look amazing in anything, or...

Nothing.

I gulped.

"Yeah," I said. "She's hot." I looked back at Cole. No point in gawking at what I couldn't have.

Silence. Good. Maybe he'd drop the subject? Nah, I quickly realized he was just reloading.

"Ya know," warned Cole, "Lucas is working on her."

A sharp pain knifed all the way down my back. Not *Lucas*, of all people. All the girls giggled and whispered when he swaggered by. Oh man, no no no – not Lucas. That conceited lug head, who always bragged about how much he could bench press? Like we cared!

"Just look, if you don't believe me," Cole challenged.

Once again, I broke down. Looked back.

There stood Lucas, staring at Emma from the opposite side of the circulation desk, leaning in, smiling, trying to work what he surely thought was his magic. Presumably, this was what Cole called flirting. Maybe it was; I could only see half her face, so it was kind of hard to gauge her reaction.

I knew one thing for sure: My stomach was churning like a pot of acid stew, and I felt sure I was going to...um, what's the word...oh yeah...puke!

"Seriously, Josh, if you don't wise up, you *will* miss your opportunity."

I wanted to punch something, hurt someone. I'd spent so much time reading about Planet Earth. Studying, preparing. I thought I knew it all. So, how come I didn't know how to handle *this* girl?

Then again, how would I explain to her where I came from? How could I be close, really close, to her, if I had to lie all the time?

No. I didn't come here for love. I came to prove that Theosians could successfully live amongst Earthlings, a theory my parents had long supported, as proud Theosian scientists, before they died.

Anything more? Anyone more?

Not in the plan.

2

EMMA

Why do I keep putting myself through such misery? Morning talks in the bathroom mirror weren't working. *Just go to work. Just go to class. Quit trying to impress him.*

I'd recite the words; I'd think about matching my nail polish with my outfit. I lifted a hand to force my wind-blown curls into submission as I stepped across hot pavement toward the library doors. Tuesday again. My stomach fluttered as if it were a room full of butterflies.

Every. Tuesday.

If only I could forget about the day when Joshua and I first met, outside the student union. I'd been waiting in line with Kaylee, all night long in fact, to score tickets to the TTYL concert.

As I rode the library elevator to the second floor, I remembered the day I met Joshua. Looking up from the makeshift tent under which Kaylee and I took cover, and nearly hyperventilating when I spotted his dark, wavy hair.

He looked so cute, so smart. Not that I can describe exactly how "smart" looks. But I know it when I see it, and Josh had it.

Some girl tripped. She spilled pens and notebooks on the pavement. And Josh – incredible Josh! – dove in to help her.

Guys just don't do that anymore, at least not at this school. And to make matters crazier, I think he went on to help everyone who was setting up a tent.

As of that day, I couldn't stop thinking about him. He looked so alert, as though naturally programmed to observe and record every detail around him. And he seemed more mature, more together, than most college guys. Yeah, I'd met a few – a few stupid ones, a few arrogant ones, some party boys and players, but no mature ones...

Until that day.

That day changed me. Now he was permanently lodged in my thoughts. And no matter how hard I tried to resist, every Tuesday, I always ended up primping and getting my hopes up, just like now. Who would have guessed we'd both end up getting part-time jobs in the library? Fate, kismet. Had to be. *I just know we're meant to be together.*

Ugh, that sounds so high-schoolish.

But I could not give up on him. Even his friend, Cole, thought we belonged together. He told me so. Sometimes he talked to *me* more than Josh. And try though I did, I just couldn't understand why Josh seemed to back away from me.

We'd talked so much that first day, and at the concert, but now he barely seemed to notice me.

The elevator bell jolted me out of my head. I straightened my top and took a deep breath, in and out.

The door finally opened and I stepped out. As I raised a hand to straighten my hair, I saw (I think) the top of Josh's head bobbing toward the break room. *Is he running away from me again?* Sighing, I gathered up my last remaining speck of pride and walked to the circulation desk to drop my books.

Mrs. Marshall, the head librarian, barreled out into the hall. My friend, Kaylee, was working in front of a library computer. Despite the pity on her face, I grabbed my lunch, heading for the break room refrigerator.

As I opened the door, I noticed Cole sitting at the lunch table shoving a cupcake into his mouth, half of it oozing out either side, as Josh leaned up against the counter. *Don't tell me he was hiding behind the candy machine. Nice.* He did glance directly at my face, then wasted no time spinning around. OK, wait. He did smile. OK, maybe just a slight grin, but I definitely spied it. Then I managed to greet them, cracking voice and all. I could have sworn Josh had been wearing a white T-shirt before. And now...a dark hoodie? *At least Cole said hello,* I thought, stepping past Josh to put my lunch into the employee fridge. *And I know Josh smiled. Why does he keep ignoring me*? As I moved back toward the door, my heart sank. Then came Cole's words:

"Hey, you have a nice day."

I stopped short. "Thanks," I returned, then glanced in Josh's direction. "You too, Josh." *WHY talk to him? Why not just eat a gallon of ice cream salted with my own tears?*

"Yep, see ya around," he whispered, barely audible, not bothering to turn and face me. Getting out of there immediately wasn't fast enough for me. Fighting back tears, I managed to return to the circulation desk, sit down, collect what remained of my breath, and begin gathering books onto a cart.

Kaylee knew to leave me alone.

3

THINKING

Just thinking about her wouldn't hurt, right? I wouldn't let it go beyond that, though. And that's a for-sure. My stomach churned, weak and bubbling with acid. I'd battled beasts on Theos. I'd survived being orphaned. I'd grown accustomed to *fear* on Theos, almost to the point where it became my friend. And now I felt...soft. I mean, come on – freaking out about a girl?? An Earthling, no less. Had I totally lost it?

I looked up to see I was alone in the break room. When did Cole leave? Coming out of my daydream, I stared down at the cup of coffee in my hand, now cold. No more steam rising from it. No more warmth on my hand.

As I stared back up at her through the glass door, thoughts about the day we met outside the student union surged into my brain. I'd remembered everyone waiting in line for concert tickets. And Cole's face as he pointed her out to me, all lit up like a Theosian starry night. As for *her* beaming face, and her sleek body, they struck me right away. Then I remembered her face being overtaken by sadness and pain as she talked to me about her ex-boyfriends. Cole said she kept dating jerks. *Why did she do that? I could show her how a guy should treat a girl. What was I saying? Hello, common sense? Please return and take back control of my brain.* Seriously, what the heck was my problem? I wasn't here for this. *Besides, I wouldn't be good for her. Walk away, Josh. Walk awa--*

"Are you OK? Josh, are you OK?"

I looked up and focused my eyes upon Kaylee.

She stood in front of me, but was bending down to look straight into my face.

"Huh? Oh, Kaylee. I'm sorry." I rubbed my eyes and glanced at the wall clock. *Twenty minutes? I've been sitting here for twenty minutes?* "What—What did you say, Kaylee?"

"I was asking if you were OK. You were like—in a daze or something."

"Yeah. I'm fine. I just—lost track of the time."

I got away from Kaylee with maximum awkwardness and minimum politeness. I then paced back to the stacks to re-shelve books the rest of the day. 546.01. 546.02. 927.67. Nope, that one goes on the third floor.

Less interesting thoughts, yeah. But also less excruciating ones.

***

Later that night, I sat at my desk. Stacks and stacks of paperbacks, magazines, and textbooks covered every flat surface. Earth data was piled high on my desk, bed, and chair, and even overflowed into our private bathroom, where it lay in piles on the floor due to a lack of space. At least our dorm room had a private bath. A shared bath would make pretending to bathe a lot harder. Not that my roommate would even notice.

He barely paid attention to anything except his girlfriend. Lately he pretty much lived in her room. I hadn't expected coed dorms when I first came to the college. Clearly my textbooks back on Theos needed updating.

And yeah, you read that correctly: Theosians don't have to bathe. Earthlings might think it's gross, but I actually never realized how cool it was until I came to Earth.

"I really need to get a storage cabinet," I said to myself.

From what I'd learned, most males didn't worry too much about messes, but I did; a major difference between Theosian and Earth males. Right now, our dorm room resembled a small bookstore. My roommate, Stemmy, short for Ty Stemmison, had a somewhat effective (if immature) tidying trick: He simply pushed the piles back over onto my side.

Humans were all so different from each other, unlike Theosians. Theos is characterized by very little variety and a lot of rules. I'm sure our strict government has a lot to do with that. But to be honest, it seems perfectly fine to me. This variety thing can be overrated. Variety leads to conflict. Me? I like to keep it simple. And conflict, no matter what we may try to tell ourselves, is never simple. And from what I hear, there's plenty of conflict on the female dorm floors. (But that's just what I hear.)

The evening flew by quickly. Stretching my arms, I unlocked my jaw into a yawn. On Theos, that's called *doonching*. It actually took me more than a year to quit slipping with Theosian words while talking. But my body had an easy time adjusting to Earth's 24-hour cycle. The changing seasons, though? Not so easy. The constant summer weather back on Theos is something I always find myself missing (or at least 75 percent of the time...).

I wiped my forehead and was surprised to see sweat on my hand. *Huh. Didn't think it was that hot.* Without giving it another thought, I slid off my shirt, leaned back in my chair, and stretched out my legs, allowing my eyes to close. My brain needed to rest for a change. Instead, it wandered, replaying the day of my escape; a familiar yet annoying memory, and one which was occurring more and more often. I could see the corridors, the bombs, and myself sweating, too, only then the sweat was all over my body. I imagined myself jumping into the escape craft. Then: such relief. The engine roared. Then: such shock.

I heard Mani giggling.

Just when I'd thought she'd outdone herself, Mani always did something a little more bizarre and crazy. I considered her my intellectual equal, but thought I'd outsmarted her this time...'til she revealed that she'd stowed herself away on my getaway craft.

We lifted off, her smile fearless, unrelenting.

"Where are we going?!" she shouted over the noise. "Wait! Don't tell me! I don't care!"

But her expression changed as we approached Earth. Sullen and stone-like, and even paste-colored. Recalling it, I felt my body tense up in my desk chair. I then pictured *her* body curled up in my arms, as we lay on the floor of the shuttle, my hand shielding her face from the electric sparks that swirled around us during and after the crash.

After the landing, her body remained close to mine. We were surrounded by twisted and broken debris. Her arms and legs were sprawled out from being thrown around: both of us were like rag dolls in a metal cage. Gosh, I hated that part of the memory: the craft on fire, my head throbbing, spinning, Mani cupping her head in her hands, the cuts and bruises all over our bodies.

No more. I pushed those thoughts away. I forced my mind forward, to the day when we parted. Bottom line: We never could figure out how to get along, just too many differences. As one big example, she constantly complained about my being too serious:

"Josha, just relax. You're always thinking, worrying. Dude, we're the first Theosians on Earth. Lay back. Enjoy."

"You just don't get it, do you? The only reason we *are* the first Theosians on Earth is because of *my* thinking, worrying, and planning."

Then she'd always sigh. "Same old Josha I knew on Theos. I thought living on Earth would change you, help you chill out. Guess I was wrong."

"I'm the same? What about you? *Someone* has to take things seriously. Every day we live on Earth puts us at risk of being discovered. You're a Theosian running around on Earth and you still don't see a need to grow up."

So, yeah...we had to go our separate ways. It was kind of sad, but I knew we'd made the right choice. Or at least we thought so at the time.

OK, enough thinking about Mani.

Thinking about the present, and my new friends, felt so much better. Cole was a great best friend to have. He always made me laugh, with all the pranks he pulled. And his never-ending sports stats were kind of impressive, particularly since they came wrapped in that bulky muscle which the girls seemed to like.

I couldn't help but smile as I pictured Emma under my closed eyelids. Uncontrollably, my muscles tightened. What a mess I was in with her. Love her, but can't love her.

The daydream fizzled. Maybe Mani was right about me thinking too much.

My cell phone buzzed, making me jump. It was the text message alert, but I didn't look just yet. My eyes did snap open, though, to near blackness. I walked toward the only light around, which was coming from the bathroom. Once inside, I stared into the mirror. My back shimmered bright gold, in contrast with the darkness.

I blinked at myself.

I glowed quite often back on Theos, especially while dating Mani. I guess I never expected to see my golden back again. I squinted, battling back some anxiety as I wondered, *What if the glow can't be hidden underneath Earthling clothes?* I couldn't even *begin* to explain that abnormality.

A second buzz from my phone. The unchecked text. I went back over to it: Cole. He apparently thought I needed to know about all the hot girls at the frat party. Nope, not really important to m--

Wait, what was this? A pic? *Holy crap, she is hot*, I thought, scanning over a curvy blond whom he'd somehow got to pose for him. I blinked, shook my head, and tossed my phone on the bed. Too late for this stuff.

The nighttime air, seeping through an open window, seemed thicker, closer, and steamier than its daytime counterpart. *How could I sleep in this humidity? How could anyone?*

I tried, though. I kept turning, tangling myself in the sheets on my Earth-made bed. Random thoughts flashed through my head. Nope, not random, actually.

Predictable.

Thoughts of Emma, one after the other after the other.

I didn't get up to look in the mirror, much less open my eyes, but I knew my back was glowing again. *Glowing...for an Earthling. Give me a break.*

By the time I did slit open my eyes, I was surprised to see morning rays, peeking through the curtains.

4

EXPLORING

Wednesday morning I hauled a storage cabinet to our dorm in the bed of my F-350. My studies of Earth had taught me to choose a vehicle carefully, for the distinct purpose of looking manly. Ironically, if these Earthlings ever saw the slim, efficient transporters back on Theos, they'd know the true meaning of "cool."

Before I made it back, goosebumps popped up all over me, covering my forearms, my upper arms, my legs. OK. This felt familiar; a sensation humans called a "sixth sense." Only, Theosians didn't *think* we sensed things. We *knew*. And right then, I felt her—Mani. No matter what I'd said, she insisted on keeping tabs on me. *I have to figure out how to get her to stop doing this.*

The farther I drove, the weaker the feeling. To my relief, it soon disappeared. *Yep, Mani, I don't have time for you. Anyway, back to more constructive thoughts: Emma, Emma, Emma...*

I lost most of the day in the task of organizing and piling books into the cabinet – real exciting stuff. At least our room looked more like something out of *College Life* magazine. On Earth, it seems they publish a magazine about everything you could imagine.

Which worked out quite nicely for an Earth-obsessed alien such as myself.

My body felt fatigued, but my mind was busy, with thoughts and more thoughts about you-know-who. You know, *really* thinking about her, the way I told myself I never would. *Sometimes I really get tired of always having to control myself. Why can't I just be 17?*

Some gate in my mind burst wide open. Crazy thoughts rushed in, uninvited. Thoughts of Emma, then thoughts of trying to get rid of thoughts of Emma, and then, something totally different – thoughts of my abilities. Or more like how I had to hide them. I felt tired of hiding them, every day. *I could of course practice invisibility, another Theosian ability, outside in the open.* Now *that* would be way cool. Inside was safer. *Better make sure Stemmy's busy first...*

Music blared through the halls as usual, growing louder as I passed each door. I walked toward Stemmy's girlfriend's room, trying (unsuccessfully) not to look into each open dorm room. I then stopped upon the sight of him sitting on a pink and purple bean bag, hunched over, and sharing earbuds as he stared into a screen with Sam, his girl. *Now, that would be a good picture to post.* A bunch of other guys were scattered around them in the Common Room.

"Hey Josh," Sam said, lifting her head to greet me. "So, you finally came out of the abyss."

Stemmy laughed. He laughed at everything she said, even if it was clearly not humorous. "Yeah, every once in a while, he climbs out from under his rock."

I laughed back, hiding my annoyance at the both of them. *OK, so I don't come out of my room much. Fitting in feels easier in smaller amounts of time.* I stared at Stemmy and the other guys from my floor, all of them so relaxed and having a good time. I felt my chest tighten. *Why can't I be that way around Earth girls, too?* I always worried about spouting out some Theosian word, or even going invisible after I sneezed or something.

"Better be careful," Sam directed at me. "You keep reading all those books and getting so smart, you'll go nuts and end up like that crazy professor with the alien stories."

All the Earthlings in the near vicinity laughed. "What professor? What alien stories?" I tried to sound nonchalant, furrowing my eyebrows, hoping to appear genuinely curious.

Stemmy said, "Didn't you hear? There's this crazy professor going around the country claiming to have proof of aliens living on Earth. Talk about a nut—"

"Yeah, totally gone," one kid said.

A blue-haired skateboarder said, "He's just trying to get famous. Some people don't care how they do it. No one will listen to him, though."

Crazy professor comparison? Aliens? That's not good. Better look into that soon. After leaning up against the door jamb in that cool way Cole always did for about six seconds, I figured I could finally get out of there. I knew Stemmy. By the looks of things, he wouldn't be back to our room for hours. I planned to have it all to myself for a while. As I walked back to our room, I couldn't help but wonder if this professor they spoke of was for real, or really a ridiculous nut.

***

As I stepped from one side to the other of our narrow room, I slid back and forth from visible to invisible, a fairly easy process. I just closed my eyes, placed two fingertips firmly against one of my temples, and filled my lungs. After a slight pause, I allowed the air to seep from my nose, like fluid through an IV drip. Now you see me; now you don't. With each breath, I faded and reappeared. Even though it was a relatively extreme thing to do, doing it didn't make me shake or feel nauseous, as opposed to when I was around Earth females.

Practicing felt so good, so normal for me. I *did* need to keep my abilities sharp. But doing this inside all the time? Boring. Outside? Oh yeah, now we're talking. I bet every human male wished he could do this. And now, the really horrible thought—I could see what Emma's up to…

Just to practice, of course.

I squeezed the steering wheel, my hands stiff and sore, slipping around corners and down side streets, maybe a little too fast, toward Emma's long, two-story dorm building, which was shaped like a train with apartment-type units. Next year, I'd definitely request one of those.

How can I think of doing this? It's like spying, right? No, I'm not really spying—I'm...practicing.

On foot, in my transparent form, I made my way to one of her windows. Above the sound of classical piano music, I could hear her breathing heavily. No need for any special Theosian abilities here. She was breathing, really hard. At first I worried, wondering if she was all right. But my concerns left quickly as I stared into the room. *I could leave. I should leave.* No matter how many times I thought those thoughts, I ended up standing right where I was. *Just a peek, right? I mean, I'm alien, not stupid.*

Once upon a time, Theosian sunsets and chemical spirals in the lab used to be my idea of beautiful. But the sight currently before my eyes definitely topped the list. I watched as she stretched and bent in a hot pink dance t-shirt, with one side hanging off the shoulder, shorts, and tights ending at her calves, probably practicing for class the next day. As her legs parted to lunge, her arm raised for balance.

Very nice.

I stepped forward to get a better look through the window, and wouldn't you just know it? I found the only twig visible for yards!

With my foot!

Judging by the immense snapping sound, it was a big one. *Now that's luck, huh?* She looked toward the window and I dodged backward, forgetting she couldn't actually see me. *When girls call guys pigs, they're right. We are. Doesn't matter what planet you come from.*

The music clicked off and she stumbled out of the room, wiping sweat from her forehead with a towel. I managed to slither around the corner for a kitchen window view, this time without announcing my arrival by breaking a tree limb. After chugging some water, she grabbed her cell phone and walked back to the living room, so I slid back to that window. I watched as she searched the contacts on her phone and sunk into an overstuffed chair. *A phone call. This is personal. I should leave. So why am I still standing here?*

"Hey," Emma exhaled. "What's up?" She paused for Kaylee's response. Her head dropped. "Yeah, I'm still bummed." She listened again. "I know, I know."

What did she know? What was Kaylee saying?

"It's not like I can just turn off my feelings for him, you know. I keep thinking about the concert in the student union, over and over again."

Oh, great. I'm sure Kaylee did her best to blast the heck out of me to Emma.

"We got along great when we were hanging together there, and then, BAM, he turns cold on me." More listening. "Yeah, I know, I know…"

Wait, what? What did she know? I winced at the memory of that day. *OK, so I panicked afterward. Ignoring her seemed like the right thing to do. I became such a jerk. I didn't want to act like that, but she didn't know that. What else could I do? Tell her, "Hey, I'm an alien. Yeah, I'm from a planet far, far away?" Yeah, that would work.*

I heard myself sigh. I then slapped both hands over my mouth…my invisible mouth. Too bad total silence wasn't one of my abilities.

5

MISLEADING

I dreamed like crazy that night, mostly about my parents. Though I'd never admitted it to myself before, I now realized they were way cooler than other Theosian parents. In one dream, I felt my mom hug me. And I saw my dad smiling. I felt warm and safe with them. I even heard my mom talk:

"You are so smart. You'll go far in the program if you work hard. Who knows, maybe you can make some changes."

She didn't have to say what she meant: changes in the rule against Theosians going to Earth.

As scientists, they'd devoted most of their lives to this. I guess it became my responsibility when they died. *Why did they have to die? They deserved to be first on Earth.*

Deep down, I wanted them to be proud. In one dream I asked, or tried to ask, *"Are you proud of me? Did I do the right thing, leaving Theos?"*

If I'd waited for the government to approve space travel to Earth, even my great-great- great grandchildren wouldn't ever see it. I knew that much. The dreams felt so real. To the point where I questioned what was real and what was a dream.

***

A new day. The heat rose from the pavement again. Customers packed the outdoor café down the street from my dorm. Ice cream and milkshake orders piled in, as I weaved around tables and caffeine-charged patrons, stopping at the only open table in sight. *Here before Cole again.* I grabbed the abandoned newspaper from the table and flipped to the sports section, only to feel my arms go cold again. I lowered my hands, laying the newspaper on the table. *Getting pretty sick of this routine.* I felt a cold breeze across the back of my neck, the hair on my arms rising. Then: goosebumps popping up again. *Where is she? Where's Mani?* I scanned each corner of the patio, only to see Cole swaggering to the table, winking at the cute waitress who always flirted with him. He always flirted back…always.

Or maybe he was the one who'd started it…

"Hey, you catch the game last--?" No time for me to respond. He leaned back in his chair, looking away from our table. "She…is…hot."

Next thing I knew it was Cole and the waitress, locked up in a feverish game of "staring and glancing away." Before I had a chance to puke, he turned back to me, eyes suddenly serious.

"Hey, about the other day in the break room: I shouldn't have gotten in your face like that."

Too bad my special Theosian abilities didn't include mind-reading. *Where's he going with this?* Apologizing wasn't his style, at least not like this. I was so focused on Cole, I barely noticed that feeling. I looked down at my arms. *Yep, still goosebumps.*

Cole's crush brought our ice cream sundaes. We had a standing order.

"Don't worry about it," I answered when we were alone again. "I deserved it. I was an idiot." I bit off some ice cream.

He nodded, chomping down on his, too. "Yeah. You were." He laughed. "Look, I'm just trying to be your friend."

I wasted no time shooting him a pissed off look. I'd worked a long time to get that expression right.

"I know," I said, smiling.

He paused, as if hoping I would continue. When I didn't, he inched further onto the edge of his seat.

Funny, I still felt her, but Mani was nowhere to be seen. Oh well, fine, let her play that game without me.

"Look, I know you don't like to talk much about your life before coming here." He shriveled up his face until his forehead looked like a Pug. "I'm just trying to understand why…"

"…I'm such an idiot?" I finished for him. Man, I hated this. *How can I be so smart and, yet, so stupid when it comes to girls?*

Immediately, he shook his head, as if against this line of conversation. "I'm sorry, man." He then went on trying to refute my *being-an-idiot* theory, but I wasn't buying it.

"No need," I said. "When it comes to girls, I'm an idiot."

Awkward silence. His sundae looked a lot bigger than mine. I knew why.

Mine might be bigger if I flirted more.

"It's your life, Josh. Totally your business. You don't have to tell me anything. I'm your friend. It's cool," he explained, all forceful and fake. *Why don't you try a little harder, dude?*

Just then, the goosebumps faded. *Good, go ahead and leave me alone, Mani.*

"You know," he added, despite having already dug himself in a hole of meaninglessness. "I'm open-minded. You don't have to worry. It's cool."

Well, there went my appetite. I set down my spoon and pushed away my bowl.

"What are you trying to say?" I asked.

Cole slid his finger up and down the edge of his spoon, then started erratically spinning it.

Come on, dude. What's the problem?

"So..." He paused. "So, you don't like girls. I mean...*I* like girls, but you don't have to like girls. What's the big deal about liking girls?" Cole babbled, picking up more speed with every word, his eyes bugging out like a Theosian drudget's. "You don't have to hide anything from me about..." He ended right there, mid-sentence, staring at me as if telepathically delivering the rest of the sentence.

Dude, I might be an alien, but I can't read minds.

But I didn't need to. I knew what he meant.

I didn't speak, though, which made him squirm all the more. He deserved it. I sat, just staring.

Wait for it. Wait for it. Then I couldn't keep it in anymore. I blurted out a great wave of laughter. It got to the point where I was actually bellowing, at which point people at nearby tables turned in our direction. *I can't believe it. He actually thinks I'm GAY.*

Cole smiled. Then frowned. He didn't get my humor. "What?" he asked. "What's so funny?"

"Man, you are hilarious. You should see your face right now." I laughed so hard, I barely remembered to breathe. Then for added drama's sake, I laughed and coughed at the same time. "Oh...man..."

Evidently deciding it might be a little funny, Cole let a reluctant laugh slip out from under his breath. "OK. So, it's not like you...like me...right?'

OK, now *that* was seriously weird, asking your friend if he has the hots for you. I laughed, again and again, and again. "No, you're really...not my...type."

When I stopped laughing, so did he. Even though he hadn't been laughing too much to begin with. A weird quiet came over us.

"Man," I said, looking at my watch. "I need to get back. I gotta study." *Did I feel that tingling again or imagine it?*

Walking away, I thought, *Emma. – Now that's my type.*

As for Cole, I kind of left him guessing, and I certainly left his mouth hanging wide open: a big, blank, department store dummy stare.

Same sex relationships are such a big deal on Earth, way different from how it is on Theos.

So hard to get used to that.

6

PRETENDING

I stared down at the rubber shower mat. Raised my hand to rub my eyes. But still, steam fogged my view. I felt the water trickle down my leg and ankle, and managed to see a line form toward the drain. Theosians never need to shower, but I'd come to realize just how good it can feel. Hot water pelted my shoulders and back. I thought about my talk with Cole in the café. *Well, I guess that's it: I came out. Or at least Cole thinks so – maybe? So maybe he'll get off my back about Emma. Emma problem solved.*

Kind of.

Out of the shower with my hair half wet, I leaned back, squinting at the sunlight beaming in our dorm window. I then chugged the last of the milk from the quart-sized carton, the only size that fit into our tiny fridge. The newspaper on my bed caught my eye. I scooped it up, reading a headline. *What the hell?* I read it twice.

Aliens Have Landed

My stomach ached, burning. Mouth dropped open. The article read:

> *Author and Professor Stanley Dowers' new book claims 80 years of proof of life on other*

*planets. Further, he reports evidence of aliens
secretly existing on Earth today.*

He sounded like a wacko, but then again, what if
he really *had* stumbled onto something? This meant
trouble—for me and Mani. Freaked out, my mind
raced. *This wasn't good, not good at all.*

I had to go and talk to her.

***

I made it just in time for lunch at Mani's high
school. I parked my truck alongside the road. After
stepping outside, it didn't take me long to spot her,
sitting on the brick wall by the entrance stairs. She
chomped on her gum, snapping it, obviously telling the
posse of girls around her some great story. They all
laughed. *No outdoor lunch periods on Theos. Lucky
Mani.*

I knew she *sensed* me nearby, but purposefully
ignored me. Too busy laughing and throwing her head
back. I slammed my truck door, tired of playing games.
Still, she didn't turn my way. Her friends did, though,
whispering, hands cupped around their mouths,
snickering like hyenas.

"Mani."

She turned in slow motion, making me wait. I tried
to ignore her dark, long hair, her perfect skin, her
bright red lips, and those smokey eyes. I refused to
notice how her black leggings and boots made her legs
look even longer.

She angled her chin higher, flashing that smug grin.

Something inside me shook. *Why could she still get to me?*

"We need to talk," I said, holding the rolled-up sheet of newspaper in my hand.

"Ooh. Looks like you're gonna spank me. Have I been a bad girl?" Behind her, the group laughed, the loudest so far.

I stepped a few paces toward her. "No, but if you don't walk with me I might change my mind." Right away, I knew how bad that sounded. Regardless, I wrapped my hand tight around her arm. She smiled back at her friends and stepped along with me, toward the other end of the school. *Yep. This was...Mani. She liked drama.*

"Hey, for once in your freakin' life, cooperate."

"OK. OK."

"I don't know how you can stand this," I said, stepping atop crunchy dry, fall leaves.

"Stand what?"

"All these—children."

"They're the same age as you and me – some older, remember?"

"Not as far as I see it."

"Mr. Maturity, huh?"

"Look, I don't have time for this crap. You need to see this." I unrolled the newspaper article and handed it to her.

She didn't bother taking it, just glanced at it. "Yeah, I saw it. He's a crazy guy. So, what about it?"

"You *know* what."

She sighed and rolled her eyes, fitting right in with the teenagers. Keeping her voice at a nice, low volume, she said, "You and I know the truth, but the rest of the world is laughing at him, wondering which mental hospital he escaped from." She made a circle with her finger around her ear, the universal gesture of craziness.

Gosh, I hated when she acted like this.

"It's not funny, Mani. This kind of thing is a threat to us."

"Threat? Josha, I'm so sick of you being so serious. You freaking out about a stupid crazy man like this makes *you* look crazy. Talk about drawing attention to yourself."

But I didn't catch most of that. For with one single word, she froze me from the inside. I did not want to be reminded of Theos. Sure, I missed it – parts of it. I missed my parents. Felt kind of alone, in fact. But that did not mean I wanted to remember, and I certainly did not want to be called Josha.

"*Joshua*," I said slowly emphasizing those last two syllables. "You know my name is Joshua now. And the threat *might* be real. The article mentions Rootstown. That's only a few miles down the highway. Too close. *Way* too close."

"Sorry, hard to break an old Theosian habit."

"And don't…" I snapped, instantly catching myself, "say that word either." I glanced in all directions for eavesdroppers.

"OK, like...big deal. The article mentions Rootstown. It also mentions 50 other cities, all over the entire United States. Anyway..." She released a giant sigh. "What do you propose we do about the article, Mr. Serious?"

"Uh huh, well, *someone* has to be serious. Cause you don't seem to have time for it. And you and I both know how these humans can be. They'll hunt us down and kill us."

"How do you know that? That's just what we were taught. But did any of our teachers, or ancestors for that matter, *really* know? They haven't set foot on Earth. Seems to me they weren't right about everything."

"We can't afford to take chances. Just be alert. Keep your eyes and ears open. If people start believing this stuff—"

"There's *always* gonna be someone who believes this crazy stuff. That's just the way it is here on Earth – their minds are built to have skepticism – and we can't stop it. But I can tell you one thing: Getting all worked up isn't gonna help."

"Just let me know if you hear of it getting any more serious. And by the way, don't be following me, unless you have a good reason."

As if it were acting independently of her brain, one side of her mouth twisted, making a dimple appear in her left cheek.

There's that shaking inside again. Stop it, Josh. She's trouble – and nothing but.

"I mean it. Wednesday, Thursday, practically every day. I'm sick of it. The only reason you should need to contact me is for the ritual, or an emergency, and in that case, we have cell phones. So text me. Otherwise, leave me alone."

She did her finest impression of an earthling pout. "Really? The only two of our kind on this planet, and we can't talk or be friends? Ever think about how lucky you are that I *did* crash your little escape party? If I wasn't here, you wouldn't have lived more than a year without the ritual, and you know it."

Yeeeaaah, friends. Like she only wants to be friends. "There was no way I could've known about our allergic reaction to the atmospheric pressure. There was nothing about it in my parents' notes. But hey – as it turned out, having another Theosian on Earth worked out, but meeting up one time a year is all that's necessary. So get this straight for once: I'm not your chauffeur. You got one free ride. That's enough for one lifetime."

Ouch. A little harsh there, Josh. But then again, I can't have her spying on me...

"OK," she said, once again clenching my insides by snapping her gum. "Whatever you want." She then leaned in, dangerously close: "But, I know what you really want, even if you won't admit it."

Don't. Move. Don't even twitch. Not an inch closer to her. She can't hear my heart pounding. She has no idea what I'm feeling inside. Lips! Stay still. Body! Stay frozen. There – is – no – reason – to – move.

She smirked, twirling a piece of her hair around a finger. Moments after turning to walk away, she decided not to let me off that easily. She paused, then turned to face me again: "Thursday? I had school all day and worked all night at the diner. It wasn't me you felt."

I sighed. It made my lungs buckle briefly. "Yeah, right. Like I believe that. No contact 'til it's time: ten days from now, no sooner."

The school bell rang: end of lunch period. She and her friends got bunched up into a group and walked over toward the school. I heard a few mumblings coming from them. Among them:

"He's hot."

Who's hot? Me? What?

"Introduce me."

They – are – talking – about – me! Yeah, Mani. I'm hot.

And you can't have me.

Mani drifted to the front of the group, then started walking ahead of them, ignoring their comments. She then subtly but surely twitched her neck, almost like she was shaking her head, but not quite. I knew what that meant.

She used to do that on Theos. In the lab.

When she was jealous of one of the other girls.

She's jealous. Ha. She's actually jealous.

Three guys, as big as Theosian garpos, tossed around a football. When it flew my way, I lifted my hand and caught it. Tossing it back, I thought about all the time these guys wasted on games and girls. I for one had much better things to do.

As I turned to walk away, I failed to see the ball shooting back in my direction. It slammed into the side of my head – my temple, to be exact. Flashes of light overtook my vision. I blinked a couple of times, trying to refocus, and looked back over at the field. There, I saw the guys all huddled together, whispering to each other.

Oh, man. Don't tell me I disappeared. Ouch. Maybe if I leave quick—

So I did just that. I turned away, pretending nothing had ever happened. The guys then stood still, watching my truck drive away.

I didn't disappear.

7

INVITING

I dreaded the next workday. Surely Cole planned on keeping our conversation just between the two of us. When I came around the corner to clock in, I fully expected to feel stared at. But no one even so much as looked up. *So far, so good.*

I made it through the first two hours...and then...like it had never stopped...it started again. *Emma.* I couldn't stop thinking about her. It seemed like every time I looked up, she was there. Stop it! STOP IT! Earthlings = Off Limits, you idiot cretin!

Dark hoodies had been saving my life lately, keeping my glowing back good and hidden. *OK, enough of this. Plan B. Ignore Emma. Human males do this: If they can't handle it, they pretend it doesn't exist.*

Seemed like a good plan to me.

Our shifts overlapped by only an hour and a half that day. Surely I could ignore her for that small length of time.

As it turned out, she seemed to have the same idea. Most of the day, I don't think I saw much more than the top of her head. That made my do-nothing plan all the more easy.

She doesn't exist...She doesn't exist...

It was just before quitting time when I looked up from my cart of books and caught Kaylee staring at me. Well, maybe "staring" isn't quite the right word. It felt more like leering, to be honest. And it didn't say "I hate you for hurting my friend" so much as "What's up with you?" In any case, I looked away, collected my belongings from my locker, and bolted for the door, hoping my do-nothing plan was not in jeopardy.

When I made it outside into the parking lot and spotted my truck, I sighed. *Mission accomplished.* My right hand clung to my keys. Walking faster than usual, I felt a sickly churning in my stomach, not unlike what I'd felt on the day of my escape. *Maybe I'm getting a little too good at escaping.*

My right hand grabbed the door handle, then I froze. A sweet voice called my name. *Damn, almost made it!*

Wait. Not Kaylee. No...Emma?

I turned to face her. She shot a smile at me, so I faked one back.

"Joshua. Can you hold up a minute?" She quickened her steps 'til she stood about three feet in front of me. Her golden hair glistened in the sun. "You look like you're in a hurry. Am I keeping you from something?"

I did my best to pretend she didn't look as good as she did. *How should I handle this? Quick, come up with something.*

But she looked...different. It's hard to explain. More—relaxed? *What's up with that?* I liked it, though. You know: not feeling like prey, fearful for my freedom, struggling to break free.

"No," I said. "It's OK. What's up?" *Is she into me or not?* I wondered what I should do. I wanted her and didn't want her at the same time. *How crazy is this?* I thought I was a smart enough guy to have figured this whole thing out by now.

"Kaylee's having this thing," she said. "It's nothing, really, just a bunch of people hanging out. Cole's coming, and most of our English class, and some others from the library here."

"Sounds fun," I lied. "When is it?" *What the heck am I saying? Get it together, dude, and fast.*

"Saturday night." She blushed. "I guess that's tomorrow night. Duh. I forgot. Even I might not be able to come."

OK, let me get this right: She's letting me know about a party, but even she can't be there. Is she lying? Playing hard to get? Backing off?

"Thanks. I'll try to make it." I cleared my throat, doing everything in my power to look cool.

She nodded and walked back into the library.

Turn away, Josh. Don't watch. Just turn away.

Nope. Couldn't.

What just happened? What a cat and mouse game! But who was the cat and who was the mouse? Somehow I ended up sitting in my truck, without having noticed my body moving to get there. *You idiot. What had I expected would happen if I kept ignoring her? Was it really so surprising that at some point she'd give up?*

I was pathetic.

So I drove home – but not before slapping the steering wheel, oh, I don't know, six, maybe seven times.

That night, Cole called:

"Hey, did you hear about Kaylee's party?"

"Yeah, Emma told me about it."

"Well, you going? What'd you tell her?"

"I told her I'd try. Why?"

After we hung up, my brain felt on fire. Then – I had it!

Of course! He thinks I'm gay. He told Emma and Kaylee. That explains everything. Should I set them straight? (Ha, straight.) I could just let Cole solve everything for me.

It did suck to feel weird with Cole. *Would a true friend let him squirm like this? But then again, if all this kept Emma from pushing for a real relationship, maybe I shouldn't complain. After all, I'm an alien; she's an Earthling, I'm seventeen, a minor by Earth's standards; she's 18.*

Like this could ever work out.

But – sigh – I didn't like lying to her. It sucked either way.

Just totally sucked.

8

EMMA

I knew he liked me only as a friend. *Well duh, he doesn't do girlfriends.*

Great. The guy I'm crushing on turns out to be gay. How'd I miss that one?

I turned from him in the parking lot. *Eyes, please don't leak all over my top.* A pain, like a knife, cut through my chest, each and every time I breathed. *At least now I know why he backed off and acted so weird.* And the party invite hid my broken heart. *I hope.*

I had to finish my shift. *Another hour at the computer*, I thought, flopping down into the chair in front of the screen. Books couldn't be late due to my crush turning out to be gay. I needed to focus.

Focus.

My fingers pressed keys while my mind did its own thing: *Did I see a confused look on his face when I invited him? And an even weirder look when I told him I might not be coming? I think he got the I'm-no-longer-pursuing-you message. So, why did he look that way? Shouldn't he be* glad *I'm no longer bothering him? He almost looked...disappointed. Nah, it couldn't be that. That wouldn't make sense. He's GAY!*

Five more book orders to process. I looked up: 20 minutes left on my shift. Turning up the speed, I finished in 10. Kaylee's shift would last another two hours. I met up with her before I left.

"How you doing?" She leaned on the counter facing me while I started clearing off my work area.

"I'm all right."

She squinted, unbelieving.

I looked at her. "Really, I'm fine." I took a deep breath. "Well, I'll *be* fine, I'm sure."

"Yeah, um, unless you plan to steal that reference book you just put in your bag, I'd say you better take it out."

Feeling like the world's biggest idiot, I took it out and put it back on the counter where it belonged.

"Don't feel so bad. The same thing happened to me in high school."

"Really?"

"Yep. I met this ridiculously cute boy at a party once. We talked and he danced in my group. I thought he was flirting. Then he uh – well, you know the ending, I guess."

"It hurts so flippin' bad. Right?"

"Ah, yeah. Like worse than anything. But eventually, I got over him. Even became friends with his boyfriend. Can you believe it?"

"No, that's hard to imagine. I couldn't do that. And to be honest, right now I can't see how I'm gonna get over this. Like, at all."

"Well, it takes time..."

Her eyes went glassy, suddenly. *She does understand.* And I don't know why, but that helped.

Then, the skin of her face became bright and her eyes widened. *Talk about a quick change in moods...*

"So," she continued, "I say we get started on that. I'm inviting lots of hot guys to my party Friday, and you *will* be there, right?"

I cringed inside, recalling how I'd told Joshua I might not be there. Kind of a little...lie? I wasn't sure why, but it felt good to lie to him. Maybe I *was* a little mad at him for not telling me himself he was gay. But then again, I guess that was kind of personal, and his call to make. *Nah, he should have told me.*

I decided to go with that.

Yes. Time to leave. I'm out of here. I picked up my belongings from the locker room and waved to Kaylee on my way out. Funny how I was eager to be off work, but dreading the downtime, or more accurately, "think and hurt time." As I walked toward my dorm room, I started with a mantra of self- talk: *Lots of hot, available guys at the party Friday. Hot guys. Hot guys, Emma.*

I did a double-take at a blond guy in the courtyard. Funny. The guys walking past me as I left the library looked a little cuter than usual. *Hmm.*

9

PARTYING

I saw Cole bending over a broken chair the next day, in one of the library study rooms. I didn't have much time before my next class, but I knew what I had to say to him shouldn't take long. *No one else in the room – great.*

I planned on this being a very private discussion...

"Hey," I bellowed out about 30 seconds in, before giving him a chance to bring up another sports team, "did you by any chance happen to mention our conversation in the café to anyone?"

He stopped what he was doing. As he looked up, his eyes turned into darts, as though looking deep for...I don't know...the right words? "Well..."

"Oh, man..."

"Hey, I felt bad. She thought there was something wrong with her, and we both know there isn't *anything* wrong with her..." This guy: He always talked fast when freaking out.

"OK, OK, I get it, but--"

"I know! I shouldn't have said anything."

I yanked the backpack from my shoulder and slammed it onto a nearby desk. Cole jumped a little. Just to make a point, I took my sweet time before I spoke again, glancing up toward the ceiling. *Now...what do I say?* OK, yeah, he'd squirmed enough.

I looked back at him, picking up where we'd left off: "Damn right you shouldn't have."

"Look, she was hurting real bad before I told her you were gay. It might not bother you, but I can't stand to see a girl cry."

"She *cried?*" I felt my stomach plopping onto my feet.

"Yeah, man. She cried. What was I supposed to do?"

I dropped the attitude, but only by a degree. "I get it. But you should have at least *told* me."

Neither of us said another word. Me because I simply refused to; him because he had none left. But I felt like a jerk. I'd hurt Emma, bad. *So, my secret mattered more than her feelings? Man, I really knew how to treat a lady, didn't I? Get it together, Josh.*

"Sorry," he said.

"Yeah, man. I know." I sighed and brought my hands to my hips. "I'm sorry, too."

So as it turned out, sexuality was a big deal here on Earth – a really big deal. But...

I just don't get that whole thing. I let him go on thinking I was gay. Not denying equals admitting. It's not like I worried about dating. I'm not here for that. Besides, that fixed everything with Emma. Not hurting Emma, that made it all worth it.

Things worse than being gay? Let's see...ummm...oh yeah:

Coming from another planet.

That was one closet I needed to stay in.

The next day seemed to drag on, but eventually the hours did pass, ushering me right to Kaylee's party. The local department store buzzed with buyers. I looked over the dummies sporting what Earthling teens considered to be cool outfits. One in particular caught my eye: He wore a dark red, almost dirty-looking shirt and a pair of washed-out jeans with ragged frays dragging on the bottom. *How is it possible that the only pants and shirt my size cover the whole mannequin? That's luck for ya. Here goes nothing...*

I slipped them both from the dummy's body as fast as I could. Turning around to head to the fitting room, I pretended to ignore the people pointing and snickering at the plastic model, who now stood proudly wearing nothing but high-tops.

I pulled and tugged at the shirt, adjusting it in the full-length mirror on the fitting room door. *Pretty nice. I look good. Who else might think so? Girl? Guy?*

Who knows my secret?

Probably every human on Earth by now.

Is the shirt dark enough? Yeah, it'll cover...just in case I get lucky.

But real luck would involve Emma, which isn't likely anymore (never was, really).

"This should be interesting," I mumbled, pausing briefly before entering Kaylee's home. Kaylee didn't live on campus. She lived with her parents and two younger sisters, all of whom were gone for the night.

Heads turned in my direction as I walked in. Music likewise drilled itself into my ears. Dozens of people were squeezed into every available room, dancing. *Wish I could dance like that. I guess human-type dancing is out for me.* When the music changed, I felt the beat through my chest.

This house, this mansion, was incredible. I saw terraces, a pool, and *so* many rooms. Talk about classy. Totally different from living in a dorm. No wonder Kaylee chose to stay put.

I spotted Kaylee and Cole sitting in a corner, sipping drinks. As "luck" would have it, the only spot open for me happened to be a seat on the opposite side of Kaylee.

Now, don't get me wrong, I knew this was her party, but did that require her to smile constantly, as if her teeth were planning an escape from her mouth?

"This place is crawling, huh?" Cole screamed to me over the music. It was a miracle I could hear him at all.

"I know, right? How did they all squeeze in? Emma said it was just going to be a few people hanging out."

"When one person, tells another person, and they tell another, and so on, you end up with one freakin' awesome party – like this." Cole looked around smiling, not making the slightest effort to hide his total awe.

Looking around, I spotted Emma across the room. Her blue dress shimmered against her skin. *Wow. Look at her*. And her hair fell across one bare shoulder...as she turned to glance at me.

I think.

Did I see her eyes light up, looking my way? Probably not. Hello! Who's that tall guy she's talking to? He really seemed into her.

She waved at me! She then leaned in to say something to Mr. Hotty, and started walking my way. I scooted over trying to create enough room for her to sit by me.

"Hey," she said.

"Hey, I said. *Major points for originality!*

"You came."

Though neither one of us could come up with much to say, she went ahead and squeezed into the seat beside me.

She seemed different, distracted, thoughtful. *What was she thinking?*

"Yeah," I answered. "I see you made it, too."

She answered with a smile. We sat and listened to everyone else talk/scream. Then we drifted into something resembling a conversation of our own, wherein neither of us could hear the other properly. I nodded. She nodded. I laughed. She laughed. But I couldn't tell you one word that was said. Meanwhile, the presence of her body beside mine made it way too hard to focus on or care about anything else. Then Emma and Kaylee had a short conversation of their own...

"Emma," Kaylee said. "There are so many guys I want you to meet tonight. Don't you dare leave without checking in with me first."

"All right, I promise," Emma said, looking my way, keeping the corners of her eyes on me.

Umm, does she or doesn't she want to meet all these guys? Why do girls have to be so tough to read?

"So," Kaylee went on. "What did you think of Brady?"

It was like the channel changed on Emma's face, turning it a shade of crimson. She looked back toward the guy she'd been talking to when I arrived, then back to Kaylee. With a shrug: "He's nice."

Was that all she thought of him? This...Brady. I didn't think I liked Brady very much. I looked over at him. Glared, in fact. Watched him stare Emma up and down, definitely doing the unthinkable in his mind's eye.

Yep. Definitely didn't like Brady.

Finally, after what had seemed like an eternity, she looked at me and spoke again: "Hey, you want to get some air?" She threw a look toward the balcony.

My brain lapsed, but I shook myself out of it. "Yeah...OK....let's go."

I followed her outside like a puppy. She sat down on a bench. Sitting down beside her, I picked up the strong scent of the flowers. Roses, Begonias, and many others whose names I didn't know, all around us. Dizziness grabbed me. I just wanted to stare at her...and...maybe kiss her. But I snapped my gaze away from her, staring at some pink flower instead. Studying each and every petal. *Focus on the flower. Don't stare at Emma. Don't stare at her hair, or her shoulder, or any freakin' part of her. Come on, Josh. Think of something cool to say.*

Anything. She cleared her throat. *Sounds cute when she does that.* "Great party." Evidently, she'd thought of something to say before me.

"Yeah, great." I paused. "Crowded."

"I know. Kaylee knows a ton of people." Silence again. She took a deep breath.

Was she...getting sick?

She turned to me. "Josh, do you remember when we first met—outside the student union?"

"Yeah, I remember." *What is this, a memory test? Where is she going with this?*

"All the fun we used to have, laughing and getting on each other, poking and teasing?"

I laughed. "Yeah, the spray cheese?"

She laughed, too. And then she stopped. Abruptly. Her face tensed. "Then the concert...so freakin' awesome."

I let my head drop. "Yeah, I remember that." I searched for more words, thought of what to say, but...nothing came to me. I then looked up to find her staring directly at me.

With—those eyes.

"I loved how we had fun back then," she said, leaning in closer. "We could be friends like that again, you know."

Aha. So this was the let's-be-friends-after-breakup speech. OK, well, technically not really a breakup since we'd never actually dated.

"OK." *Brilliant! Colossal! How did I come up with these amazing lines?*

"Let's get everything out in the open. It's obvious that I like you. But Cole told me everything and I understand. None of it matters to me. All I care is that we're friends."

Just like that...that was it. She seemed finished with her speech.

Wow. Such honesty. That took guts. Just what I needed, more reasons to like the girl I couldn't ever have.

Just then, a breeze blew into her curls. She lifted a hand to catch them.

"No, don't. Your hair looks great." *Did I just really say that? Whoa, getting good at this whole "gay" routine.*

She looked at me and grinned, then looked away.

Start talking again. No silence. No staring. What were we talking about? Oh yeah:

"You're right. Friends. That's all that matters."

She smiled, then wove her arm around mine.

Just then, Kaylee yelled from inside the house, popping our happy bubble:

"Emma, get in here! I have someone I want you to meet!"

She looked at me with sad eyes. "Sorry, I promised her."

"Yeah, I understand."

But that was just another lie. I didn't understand anything. Valuable Lesson: Life on Earth doesn't necessarily make sense.

I wasn't really sure it ever would.

10

GIVING

The next day, at the library, I struggled with the combination on my locker. *Why does that happen every time I'm in a hurry? What's that stuff Cole uses? What's it called?*

Oil, I think. Maybe that would help.

Opening the door, I moved to fling my jacket inside and stopped short at a weird sight: a clear vase filled with yellow daisies, down there on my locker's bottom surface. *What the heck? Flowers? No one ever gave me flowers before. Isn't that what human males give to females? Why was I getting flowers? Oh, man. Could they be from...a guy?* My hand shook slightly as I reached for the card.

It read: *I'm so glad we're friends again.*

I felt a finger tickling my rib-cage.

She laughed when I jumped, slightly startled. "That's quite a look on your face," she said.

"Thank you—but, you shouldn't have done this."

Her smile started waning. "I wanted to."

"They're really nice, but to be honest, I'm not sure what to say if someone sees them and asks who got them for me."

Wait, am I hurting her? How would you tell a girl that it's not right to give a guy flowers? I'm so weirded out right now.

"I didn't think of that," she said. Her head dropped. What remained of the smile melted from her lips. "Well, we're the only three that know. Well, wait— make that four. I told Kaylee."

Great. Another person thinks I'm gay. Just what I wanted.

Then she dropped a bomb: "I know!" she gasped. "Tell everyone we're dating."

I can't really say how long I stood there staring at her with my mouth hanging open. *What? Close your mouth, dude. She's serious. Say something. Anything.*

"Josh, did you hear me?"

"Uh…yeah…I heard you."

"We can make it really convincing. We can hold hands and maybe even kiss in front of people." She giggled. "What do you think?"

Like I was capable of saying no to that!

11

FOOLING

"That…yeah…that'd be cool."

Did she just offer to pretend to be my girlfriend? Well, uh, yeah – I could go for that! I smiled at her. She smiled back. *Oh yeah, those lips. I want to kiss them all the time now. Can she tell?* "But you don't have to do that." *Had I sounded convincing?*

"It's no problem." She laughed a little, then looked down, seeming embarrassed.

"What?" I asked.

"Oh, it's nothing." She grabbed her name-tag from her locker and slammed it shut.

"No secrets." I shot a grin at her.

Mercifully, she grinned back: "You'll laugh."

"No, I won't. I promise."

She paused, then looked up at me again. "It's just that…you…I mean…you're the perfect friend." She sighed. "I so need a boyfriend that knows how to be a good friend, too. Guys are just—so stupid. Sometimes I think they're from another planet, you know?" She shook her head. "I can't explain it."

"Sounds like a good explanation to me."

She looked straight into my eyes. Everything and everybody else around seemed to disappear. We were the only two people on the planet. Her planet.

"Hey," I said, afraid of saying or doing something really stupid if I stayed put. "We should probably get back to work. It's Sunday; only a few short hours today."

Her shift was about over, in fact. And every bit of knowledge I had about Earth told me to close my locker to hide the very *unmanly* flowers. So I did.

She looked at me. Then:

"OK if I just keep them in my locker for now?"

"Yeah," she agreed. "That's cool."

"I'd, uh, rather Cole not see them."

"Oh—yeah. He would never let you live that down."

"Yeah, he'd be merciless." *Phew. She's so cool.*

I gestured my hand for her to walk first. I followed behind, her lovesick puppy. *Did I stare at her too long? Does she suspect anything?* That's it. No more looking into her eyes from now on…if that's possible.

12

PROTECTING

I sniffed the cool morning air. The breeze made my jacket swell like a balloon. The changing colors of the leaves was so awesome, something I'd never seen on Theos, where it stayed summer all year long. *So boring,* I thought as I pulled a paper from my pocket.

I looked down at my schedule, which included Calculus III and Chemistry II, with a little disappointment. I'd tried not to do well on the placement tests, but I guess I hadn't tried hard enough. I actually tested out of Calculus I and II.

Meanwhile, the college also required speech, English, and United States history. *Already learned each of these back on Theos.* I was usually bored out of my mind in class, but then again, ironically, it was the one place I felt most at home. It reminded me of my days as a student on Theos, learning something new every day. I missed it a little: the smell of chemicals boiling in the lab, the video learning screens with adjustable speed. *These Earth professors teach way too slowly. Wish I could turn up their speed.*

I only looked forward to one thing more: time with Emma. Some days we spent our entire lunch breaks together, just talking. Thanks to work, class, and studying, lunch was seeming to be our only true free time together.

One day at noon, Cole side-swiped me, taking me out of the classroom, down the hall, down two flights of steps, and out the door. "Hey!" I protested. "I'm meeting Emma for lunch."

"What's this I heard about you and Emma going out? Excuse me, but wasn't it my understanding you preferred someone more, uh, masculine?" He looked around as he spoke to make sure no one overheard.

Why was this such a big deal to him?

"Cole, calm down," I said with a laugh. "Emma just agreed to pretend we were dating to protect my secret.*" And boy, did I have a secret to protect. If only he knew...*

"Ohhh." He didn't seem to realize how long and far he drew out that word. "I see. Pretty clever. Dude! You wouldn't believe the rumors flying around. Lucy, in circulation, said she saw you guys making out, and Lucas! Oh man, he's pissed as hell. He thinks you moved in on her."

"Oh, that's mature. Idiot."

"What? Wouldn't you be mad if some guy moved in on your girl?"

"I get it," I snapped, feeling exposed, "but it's not as if we're *really* dating." I'd really hoped this would calm things down. *Why wasn't it working?*

"But everyone thinks you are. So you might as well accept it: You are."

"Whatever" was my comeback. *But then again, what could I do about Lucas? Women on Earth are seen by some guys as territory? I don't get it.*

Back in the hallway, Lucas leered. Didn't speak. Didn't even come close to me. Just leered. I walked past, to where Emma sat, working at the computer behind the reference desk.

Upon seeing me, she called me over with a quiet "Psst." Started to tell me about Lucas.

"He kind of scared me," Emma said. "He kept saying I was too good for you over and over again, and that he would prove it to me. I told him to back off. He just kept it up and kept it up until one of the girls called my phone and said I was wanted in the office."

I started burning – all over my body, under my skin. My hands twitched, then balled up into fists. And my head began to throb. But I didn't want Emma to see me angry. I *couldn't* get angry. Couldn't let myself. I'd only let that happen a couple times in my life. When I needed to protect myself. *Control. Control. Don't kill Lucas. That will complicate things.*

"I'll take care of it," I said.

"No, don't do anything."

"Don't worry. I'll get it all straightened out."

Before she could protest again, I made tracks for Lucas' desk in the Math lab, down on the bottom floor. I imagined the bottoms of my shoes digging into the carpet. They didn't, really; it just felt like it. And I tried breathing deeply as I took each step, but it didn't make me any calmer. In fact, I just felt warmer and warmer. Beads of sweat formed on my forehead, already beginning to drip down the side of my face, past my eyes. I stood in front of his desk, still as a statue, 'til he looked up.

"What do you want?" His voice made the fire blazing in my head even hotter.

"Outside."

After a second's pause, which he filled with staring, he rose, then walked with me up the stairs and outside. I followed closely on his heels. From behind, I pictured myself grabbing him by that perfectly styled hair of his. I *so* wanted to do that. Once beyond the glass doors, we stopped and faced each other. With our noses only inches apart, we stared each other down for minutes which seemed more like hours.

Then I said what I'd come to say: "I don't care if you're pissed at me. You and I can go, right here, right now, anytime, anywhere, I don't care...but you will *not* take it out on Emma."

"You don't deserve her. What business do you have moving in on *my* girl?"

"From what I saw, you weren't getting anywhere with her."

He let out some sound between a snarl and a growl.

"I'm not surprised. She doesn't waste her time on players."

Success! He drew back his fist and wailed it at my chin. I blocked his shot easily, pushing him against the brick wall, pinning him so hard I could tell he was having a hard time breathing. Jerking and gasping, he took me in with big, shocked eyes. Tried to push me away. Couldn't break free. He just looked at me, eyes bulging to the point where it seemed like they could burst. I held him there just long enough to get my point across, then I pulled him slightly away from the wall and, with a forceful push, let go, smashing his body against it, one more time, just for fun.

A smart guy would have ran right then and there, but not this mindless oaf. He grabbed a breath and tried coming at me again. This time, I wasn't so patient. I nailed his nose with my right fist, followed by his stomach with my left. Watched him crumble to the ground like a demolished building, which was amazing since I was holding back most of my strength. *Dude, you do not know who you're dealing with. Don't make me use my real strength.*

He stayed doubled over on the ground this time, moaning and holding his nose as blood dripped between his fingers. I turned and, without once looking back, walked back inside the library and to the locker room, my body cooling as I tried to pretend it never happened.

But my sore knuckles made that kind of hard – *oww*.

About a hundred owws later, Emma rushed in, breathing hard.

"Josh," she said. She blinked back tears. "Did you have to hurt him?"

"You saw?" *Wait. Is she about to cry? For him? For me?*

"From the window."

Wait. What? She's mad at me, for protecting her?
"Emma, someone needed to teach him a lesson. I did what I had to do." I stood up and moved closer to her, so no one would hear. "He won't bother you again. If

he ever comes near you, let me know. Nobody's gonna mess with my girl!" It was meant to be a joke, more or less, and I made sure to cap the statement off with a playful wink.

But, I must admit, it had felt good, real good.

So why didn't she look happy? What had I done wrong?

As it turned out, I was right: He didn't bother her again. He stayed far clear of me, in fact, apparently preferring the ability to breathe to its opposite. Cole made jokes about my being a badass around the library, pretending to flinch and draw fists whenever I'd enter a room.

"You the library bully, man. No one gonna mess with you."

Irony of ironies, if they could see what I *really* had in me, they wouldn't be laughing, they'd be scared – especially Emma.

But I can't ever hurt her. I love her. Naturally, I said that in my head only. *Love sucks. It's never worked before, so why would I bother now...and with a human?*

13

EMMA

I stared out through the second story window. Down on the pavement below, Joshua and Lucas were staring each other down. *Why was he going to fight, for me? Lucas was definitely a jerk, but if Josh likes guys, why did he care so much if Lucas had a thing for me? And why did I say I was scared of him? I could have taken care of myself! I know Josh is just my friend but, come on. He acts like he kind of...likes me—but Cole said he was gay!*

I stood watching—cringing—as Josh deflected Lucas' punch and pinned him up against the brick wall. Until he released him, I was unaware that I'd been holding my breath. I sucked in some air. *Lucas, you idiot. You're coming back for more? Josh, just let him go--*

Uh, oh. Well, there it was: one to the nose and another to the stomach, and down Lucas went. On sheer principle, I hated to see people bleed, even if it was jerk blood.

I met up with Josh in the break room. He rubbed his sore knuckles. I saw their redness and flinched.

"Josh, did you have to hurt him?" I gulped down, fighting back tears of – I don't know what. Frustration? Confusion? You name it.

"Emma, I did what I had to do." He furrowed his brow. "Besides, no one will ever mess with *my* girl."

Then came a quick little wink. He must have been joking but—that look in his eyes. I knew that look. Every girl knew that look. He turned and walked out of the room, leaving me standing there, writhing inside. I tried to get ahold of myself. *He's gay. Cole knew, right? But, his look – it melted me.* I searched the depths of my brain for some sort of answer. *What am I supposed to think? Maybe he's bi*, I thought, a jolt running through me.

Well, there's only one way to find out...

14

SHARING

Hanging with Emma was the height of coolness. *Who needs lunch when you can just look at her face for an hour?* Nothing else around me mattered. I hardly even noticed her fingers clanking on my computer keyboard.

"So, how do you want your title page, single- or double-spaced?"

"Huh—oh—um—single." Then, like an idiot, I added, "Like me."

Emma blushed a little, then kept on typing.

I could have typed faster myself, 230 Earth words per minute actually, but that wasn't something I was in any rush to share. Besides, she wanted to help, as a thank you for getting Lucas off her back. Letting her help was the least I could do, right?

Although I'd never had this problem before, focusing on homework took much more effort now. Her smooth legs, peeking out from beneath plaid shorts, were like magnets to my eyes, all soft and shiny. I worked hard not to let her catch me staring. But as she leaned over to ask about words and phrases, whiffs of her perfume spiked up my nose, making me almost cross-eyed. OK, I'd have to work *way* harder on the subtlety of my reactions.

Back on Theos, I'd once read a book that mentioned something called "friends with benefits." I thought very little about it then, but right about now, that concept was starting to sound pretty good.

As these sessions accumulated, I struggled to keep my eyes in my textbooks. Focused or not, the good grades came, which never ceased to impress Emma.

"Another 99%? You're too freakin' smart," she'd smile.

If Emma was happy, I was happy. And getting my daily fix of her made me happiest of all.

As a matter of course, she'd ask for breaks. I never objected, though I never, ever needed one.

"My brain hurts. I need a break." Emma sighed, rising to stretch.

I noticed she would talk, *really* talk, to me during these breaks, so I made sure to make them last. Which meant making sure to bring along plenty of her favorite snacks.

She eyed the bag. "Oooo. Oh yeah. Corn chips." She tore the bag open, digging into them.

"My mom says I attract the wrong kind of guy," she said. "It got to the point that I started believing that was all I could get."

"You don't really believe that, do you?" I handed her a can of pop.

She cracked open its lid. "I would like to say no, but I guess I'm not real sure," she said, her eyes aimed down. She aimed her eyes down way too often. This time, she capped it off by shoving a chip into her mouth.

"Oh, come on now. You deserve a really great guy." At that moment, I asked myself exactly what I was doing. *Yeah, he's out there, that's for sure, and not too far away either.* Then it came: the pain. So much of it. *This really sucks.*

"Sometimes I believe it. But other times, I'm afraid I'll never meet him. Besides, with men being from Mars and women from Venus—or is it the other way around?"

"Neither, actually."

"What did you say?"

Oh, crap. "I mean, I wouldn't worry about all that." *What the hell was that supposed to mean?* "You'll meet him, I'm sure of that." A part of me wondered who was talking right then. Whoever he was, he was stupid. *Shut up, Josh. Shut up.*

"Thanks, Josh," she said, leaning in a little closer. "You're a great friend." She flipped her car keys through her fingers, letting her sister's picture briefly flash into sight. She looked down at it, too, smiling. "My little sister is better at choosing guys than I am. I wish I had better judgment, back then and now."

Every time she called me a friend—and she did that a lot, I was noticing—a knife-like pain stabbed my gut, followed by the inevitable relief that I didn't have to tell her I was an alien. Ever since Mani and I had—well, yeah, I guess I needed a break after that whole thing.

How stupid I'd been, to have once believed Mani was the one. Anyway, I fell for her, hard, and when it was over, I was burned. I really liked Emma, but it would never work. My being an alien was in the way, for one thing, and for another thing my heart couldn't handle another hard hit. That is, what Mani had left of it.

I'm not sure why, but one night I found myself telling Emma about her, minus some details here and there.

"There was this girl I dated," I explained slowly, as the two of us relaxed on the couch. "It didn't work out."

"You mean you *did* date a girl? And after that you discovered you were gay?" She released some air, having gone to the trouble of choosing her words very carefully.

"Yeah, um, no. Well: Can we skip the whole gay thing for right now?" *Great, now what does she think?*

"Oh, I'm sorry," she said, her eyes wide, almost flashing fear.

"It's OK." I pushed forward: "I'm not sure if this makes any sense to you, but I thought she was the one, just like you thought with each of those *wrong* guys."

"I did. I felt so sure about every one of them."

"That's what I mean. I know it's a cliché, but love really can be blind." *Did I get that saying right?* I must have. She didn't laugh at me. Just think, *I was giving her* relationship advice; what a hypocrite. "I'm no expert, but it seems to me you have to think about what you want from a relationship. "

"I get it," she said. "That's how I know the kind of friendship you and I have is exactly what I want—I mean—the kind I want to find." The tail end of her

75

sentence kind of got tacked on as an afterthought. As for the first part, it hung there in the air, radiating pure confusion.

The room darkened as the sun set, leaving ambiguous shadows on every wall. It suddenly became quiet—almost romantically so. Inches separated us on the couch, but they felt like miles. Our eyes met, over and over, briefly. Each time, we both glanced away. My eyes didn't want to, but I made them. I can't speak for hers.

"Friendship and love can be good together," I muttered. *I want this conversation. Yet, no, I don't.*

She sat quiet, yet I felt the swell of all her unasked and unanswered questions. *I think I know what she was trying to say. Or am I crazy?* The tension felt heavy, as did my chest. I decided to appease her mind a little. "Emma, I'm a very—complicated pers—"

"It's OK," she interrupted. "You don't have to explain anything to me. It's really none of my business."

"I know I don't *have* to tell you anything. I want to." I took a very deep breath. It almost hurt. Suddenly, random words were spilling out my mouth, splattering all over the little patch of air in between us: "My life is filled with a lot of weird stuff. It's too hard to explain. But I want you to know that if I *could* have a relationship with someone, you would make a pretty good choice." *Make a pretty good choice? What kind of idiot am I?* I read the confusion on her face. So once again, for some reason, I just let the words roll out of my mouth, and probably not the best words I could have chosen for that matter: "Leaving out all the gay stuff, um, there are so many reasons, uh, I can't be with you. But you deserve a very special guy, one that will treat you right."

Her smile made me smile. All of that was short-lived, however, as the sides of her lips sank downward almost immediately.

"I wish you could be that guy," she whispered. "I'm not gonna lie and say I understand because I don't, but I do trust you. I'm only gonna say one more thing about it, and then I need to get going."

"OK, what?"

Shadows danced upon the walls around us. Both of our voices had softened now, almost to a whisper.

She leaned in to speak. "Be very sure of your decisions."

I frowned for some reason. The expression simply took hold. I felt hurt, but wasn't sure if that was the appropriate reaction. In any case, I didn't speak.

"*You* might be the one that's blind," she explained. "If a person can be wrong in thinking a relationship *will* work, can't it be the other way around, too? You know—assuming one *won't* work. If you think about it, it makes sense."

She looked smug, something I'd never seen on her, and after she got up and left, I just sat there, staring at the wall. *Why did she have to go and say that? If only she knew the truth about me, she wouldn't be talking like that.*

No, her only thoughts in that case would involve turning and running off, as quickly and as far away as possible.

During the next few days, Emma's words from that night kept repeating in my head. Could she be right? If I followed my heart now, she'd think she turned me. If I told her I never was gay, she'd maybe (very rightfully) hate me for lying.

I mean, *I* hated me for lying.

My constant thinking made it nearly impossible for me to focus at work, even with my ridiculously simple job. *Could she be right? Should I follow my heart? I can't date a human. I just can't...even if I think I...love her. Plus, I'm 17, a minor. She's 18, an adult. On Earth, that's just wrong.*

Right?

While I was lost, as usual, in the thicket of my problems, Cole came up behind me in the hallway.

"Hey, bud." His voice made me jump a little.

I didn't turn. "Hi, Cole." I shelved a book: *Fundamental Concepts in Algebra.*

"Hey, how's it going with Emma?" he asked.

Now I turned. He gave me a wink and a grin.

"It's good."

"Yeah, it must be. I don't see you anymore, except here." He lowered his voice. "If I didn't know better, I'd say you were really falling for her."

I didn't respond. Just gave him a look.

"Well, you two *are* together all the time." He raised and lowered his eyebrows quickly, making them look like they were doing some fancy jump-and-land. "You even look at each other funny."

"Come on, she's just doing my typing. Don't be stupid."

"Yeah...I know. That's stupid. But I kind of want to talk to you about her." He spoke cautiously now; his words moved slower. "There's kind of a situation. I don't really know how to say it."

"Just spit it out." Truly oblivious, I continued doing my best to organize books.

"I don't want to start a fight. And I hope you don't get mad at me. It's just that...I kind of...like her."

I eyed him. He looked at me sideways, gauging my reaction.

"What do you mean, you like her?" I asked, emphasizing each word. I squeezed the book I held between my hands. *Trigonometry Can Be Fun.*

Yeah, sounds a lot more fun than what I'm doing...

"I like her, Josh." The speed of his words picked up again. Good old Cole: get nervous, talk fast. "I know she's your cover and all, and I didn't mean for this to happen. It just—happened."

My blood felt like it was bending my veins. I didn't know what to say to him. Temperature was rising; fists were clenching.

My best friend has feelings for the girl I secretly love?

PART TWO

This can't really be happening, I thought. But it was.

15

REFUSING

A pressure, like a steel beam against my chest, crushed me, leaving me unable to catch my breath, let alone respond. That in mind, turning away from him seemed the best choice. OK, maybe not the best, but that's what I did. If I looked at him, well...there was no telling what I might do. His voice trembled, especially with his last three words. "It just—happened." Three words I simply could not accept. Those things don't *just happen*. A person *knows* what's happening. And they can stop it from happening. The pain in my stomach reminded me of my own guilt. *But could a person really control falling in love?*

Could I?

He stood still, not speaking—smart move on his part. I stepped away a few steps, exactly the opposite of what I wanted to do.

I'd much rather have yelled at him, told him I wasn't gay. Gah, I'd almost told Emma. Almost.

Cole's silence actually gave me a little time to think. *Now what do I do?* I rubbed my forehead; its pulsing veins gave my fingertips tiny kisses. *Enough thinking. Don't make this harder than it needs to be.* At long last, I turned back to face him.

"No." *Shorter response than you expected*? I stared Cole down. Fire burned in my head. At least it *felt* like fire.

"What do you mean, n*o*?"

I felt my body straighten, like someone had pulled a string up from the top of my back—like I was a puppet.

"No, I don't want you to see her." *Really? You're telling him not to see her and expecting him to agree?*

I needed to stay under control.

"I don't understand." He flung his hands up into the air and turned away. Then: "So, you're monopolizing both genders?" He paused, facing me. "I wasn't asking. I was telling. And I didn't even have to do that. Josh, I...like...her."

His last three words clanged in my mind. I imagined lasers shooting from my eyes, and cutting into his. The ache in my head turned to pounding. Every muscle in my body felt so tight, rigid.

"I'll say it one more time." I paused in order to take a much needed breath (plus I also got some mileage out of the dramatic affect). "Don't do it. I'm warning you. Don't do it."

So this is what ego and testosterone feel like. I saw his forehead crinkle. *I'm getting to him. You won't see me cracking, dude...*

Point made. I turned and walked away. It had felt good, standing up for myself, and letting out my real feelings for once. *Freedom. Feels nice. Hey, I didn't escape from Theos in a spacecraft to pretend away my life on Earth. Shouldn't this gay charade be ending sometime?* My feet glided smooth across the floor. I walked increasingly taller, allowing myself a touch of swagger. *So what if I'm terrified and have no solid plan of action?*

I feel pretty damn good.

I'll tell you one thing: He's not *stealing my Emma time. I want more than just lunch with her. My best friend isn't going to steal my girl.*

"Here," I said to her. "Let me help you with that?"

Emma sat on my couch. Her little legs were crossed together Indian- style, shoes on the floor in front of her. She slouched over her Analytical Geometry book.

"You help me all the time with typing. My turn."

She sighed, surrendering, sliding the book my way as I sat down beside her. I studied the page briefly. "OK, for these types of problems you use this formula." I pointed to a particular patch of text.

"I know. I was trying." She showed me her calculations.

I studied them. It only took a moment. "You're on the right track. You only did one thing wrong, not carrying over this number from this step to this step. See?"

She hovered close to me. *Good: She doesn't know what's up with Cole. And I'm not about to be the messenger.*

"Oh, I didn't even see that." She looked up, smiled, then grabbed the paper, erasing and fixing her mistake.

Seeing her all the time felt so good. I almost forgot about...being an alien.

As if worrying about how to make things work with Emma wasn't enough, I had to start obsessing over ruining my friendship with Cole. Meanwhile, he avoided me. And I avoided him. But that all ended two days after our threatening little encounter, when I spotted him while walking through campus between classes. He slowed his pace as we approached each other. So I did, too.

"Hey, Josh. How's it going?"

"Good. Yourself?"

"I'm good." *Will he back down? Will I? Well, he is the bigger person, literally. And definitely more muscular. He thought he could have pounded me the other day, I'm sure. But it was really me holding back.*

"You catch that game last night?"

Ah, Cole's sports-filled conversation. I actually missed this stuff...

"No, but I heard about that bad call." Within moments, I came to learn that talking sports was some Earthling male ritual that existed in place of apologies.

"Yeah, it was brutal." He looked down at the books I carried against my leg. "Calc?"

"Yeah. Just left it. On my way to Chem."

"OK, well. I'll let you go."

"Right. See ya." I started to step away.

"We should hang sometime," he added.

"Yeah. Text me." *Hmm, part of the ritual involves walking away while still talking...*
"Will do."
And that was that.

16

ADMITTING

Another night, another homework-filled session with Emma, this time an English paper. I tried to forget Cole, without success. *But Emma's not mentioning Cole. Is he standing down?* My stomach jittered; I found myself talking constantly. I talked about everything, in fact—except, of course, for what was really bothering me.

Act normal, Josh. Oh man, I'm so nervous. I'm not even sure what freakin' normal is. Don't ask me about it, Emma. Oh no – I can feel her, staring at me. Do. Not. Ask. If she knows, she sure is being cool about it.

At the end of the session, as she rose to leave, I lingered behind her, thinking I might actually just go ahead and blurt it out. She hesitated at the door, looked at me. Those amazing hazel-colored eyes beamed right through me, in fact.

"Josh, are you feeling all right?"

"Yeah. Why? Do I look sick?"

"Sick. Upset. Something."

"Cole's mad at me." *Wow. I said it.* I looked at the floor and shook my head, my hands shoved deep into jean pockets.

"Yeah, I wondered. Did you guys talk it out yet?"

"No, not really." I tried to push away a little twinge of guilt, and failed. After all, she still didn't know the problem, which was significant seeing as it was *her*. "But, I saw him on campus the other day. I don't know. I'm still trying to work it all out in my head."

"Wait a minute. The guy who writes amazing essays and papers can't find the right words? Impossible." She smiled.

"School papers are easy. Real life isn't."

"I know what you mean. Life can suck sometimes."

"You got that right." I had to force myself to use improper grammar, imitating the way those around me spoke. Once again, I let her walk out that door, without managing to come clean. *Wrong choice, Josh.* Pacing around the room for the next half-hour, I only managed to mentally confirm my mistake. In time, without thinking, I picked up my phone, squeezing the life out of it in anger, and pushed her name on my contact list. *I can't be a chicken. Now or never. Do it!*

"Hello?" Her voice made my heart speed up.

"Emma, I know it's crazy to call, since you were just here all evening, but there *is* something I need to talk to you about. Um…but if it's too late…maybe tomorrow—

"No. It's not too late. On the phone or in person?"

No matter how hard I tried, I just could not manage to believe how nice she always was to me. *Was that a little excitement I detected in her voice? No. Couldn't be.*

I walked into her dorm room spewing apologies, but she quickly pushed them aside.

"Stop apologizing and get in here." She grabbed my sleeve and yanked me through the doorway. Then she sat on the edge of her bed, waiting patiently (it seemed) for me to begin.

I plopped onto a pink futon. One deep breath. *Here I go.*

17

EXPLAINING

I blinked, taking in all the *pink* in her room. A lot of Earth females seemed to like pink. Gender-specific colors didn't exist on Theos.

"This is awkward," I said, stating the obvious. "I hated to bother you after you just spent *all* night working on my stuff."

"I'm glad you called. Honestly, I've been worried about you. I could tell something was up..."

"Well, I think it's time I tell you what's going on." I searched her face. *What are you thinking? No clue. Go. Go. Go. Say it!* "There are some things I should have told you."

"OK, like what?"

"Wow." I laughed, very deep under my breath. "There's a lot, actually." I leaned forward, my hands folded in front of me. My eyes found a spot on the carpet—pink, of course—and focused on it, as if it could miraculously tell me what words to choose. "I wish I knew where to start."

At that moment, she touched my hand with hers, ever so lightly. *Did that electrical current run through her body, too?*

"Just start anywhere. You don't have to tell me everything."

Once she finds out, she'll hate me. I'll lose her. I just know *I'll lose her. Maybe there's a way to keep her.* "It's about me—and my past. I know you say I don't have to tell you, but you're wrong. I do. I need to tell someone." *I wish I could tell her everything.*

I heard loud voices bellowing outside, in the hallway. A door slammed. Then the voices faded.

"I'm listening."

I took a deep breath: in and out. "I told you that I'm not from around here. I didn't tell you where I was from, because—it's hard to explain. But, there's a lot in my past." I struggled to find each and every word. *I'm babbling.* "The first part, you already know. There was a girl I knew—and loved. It didn't work out and—it killed me. Now...this is the touchy part..."

She swallowed and re-positioned her feet, the better to brace herself, I presumed. I looked into her round, brown eyes, trying to accept that this might be my last time. "Cole assumed I was gay and I let him think it was true. I shouldn't have done that."

Nothing. Silence. Not a word, not a twinge of surprise on her face. *Waaay too much silence, for way too long.*

Finally, she opened her mouth to respond. "So, you aren't gay?" She paused, forehead crinkling, appearing to process what I'd just said. "You're bisexual?"

Her reasoning made sense, too much sense. "No, I am definitely monchue—I mean heterosexual." *Crap. I hadn't slipped up with a Theosian word for a very long time.* I stopped, letting her digest this news. *What are you thinking? I can't read your face. This feels crazy!*

"And Cole told me you're gay, because he really thinks you are?"

"Yeah," I said, frowning. "He thinks I am. You're the first person to know I'm not."

"Why on Earth would you let him think such a thing?"

"On Earth." Ha. "I don't know how to explain it completely, but…" I looked to the side, away from her, took another deep breath, and just jumped into it: "I like you, Emma. I have for some time. But I didn't act like it, because, well—for a lot of reasons. The easiest one to understand is because I don't feel that I *can* have a relationship with an—anybody." *Phew! That was close, almost said, "An Earthling."*

I never expected what came next:

"It's all right. Don't worry about it."

I don't get it. I lied to her, and she's all right with it? What's going on here?

"I like you too. But I guess you already knew that." There her head went, dropping again.

Oh. Oh, man. She likes me. She likes me! *Not Cole. Me! Stay still. Don't move. Don't run down the hall, screaming. Don't be—an idiot, Josh.*

"So, all of this…this whole gay 'act'…wasn't because you don't like me? You sure had me convinced. You really looked like you didn't like me."

I grabbed her hands with both of mine, squeezing them tightly. Shaking my head. I answered in quick, pressured words: "No, that's not true. I like you. I *really* like you." I stared at her, taking in every second of the moment I'd thought would never come. I began to fight the urge to kiss her. "You don't hate me—for lying to you?"

"Never." Just before a tear dropped from her eyes, she dropped her head again.

I reached over and lifted her chin with two fingertips. "I've been so awful to you, and dumb, very, very dumb. You have to believe me. I didn't know what to do."

"I don't understand. If you like me, and I like you, then…"

"It's not that simple."

"It's not?"

When she put it like that… "I wish that was all there was to it." I stared at her, just stared at her—the shape of her face, color of her skin, those full, red, lips. *I need to kiss her!*

"I don't understand. It makes perfect sense that I like you. You are a great person. You're smart, hardworking…"

"And many more things, things you don't know." *Let's see, I'm an alien. I'm a minor—*

"I know all I need to know. I know how I feel about you. And now I know how you feel about me. That's all I care to know."

Don't, Josh. Don't do it. I lost my head. I reached out, lifting her chin with five fingers, and leaned in closer to her, setting our lips dangerously close. I stopped for a moment, maybe waiting to see if she would stop me, thinking she would and hoping she wouldn't, all at the same time. I leaned in even closer, 'til my lips met hers. At first, it felt soft and gentle, then hard, our lips smashing together, with no possible way for us to be any closer. I felt stunned, not knowing I was still capable of such feeling, such passion.

I don't care what time it is, or about Cole, or about anything, except kissing Emma. But soon our lips parted, suddenly, both of us, as we gasped for air, smiling. Afterward, I stared into her eyes for the millionth time. My hands reached for hers, my thumbs rubbing across her skin. *I'm in way, way over my head. Falling in love—not the plan. But, I don't care anymore. I love her. This is perfect.*

Or it *was* perfect, that is, until I felt that *other* feeling again.

Oh no, Mani.

18

CONFRONTING

No, not now. Anytime but now. I can't believe you, Mani. I backed away from Emma.

"Josh. What is it? What's wrong?"

I need to slow down. What am I doing? I shouldn't have kissed her. My back's gotta be glowing like the sun. I have to get out of here!

"I better go now."

"What…I don't…Why?"

Finding out I'm straight doesn't phase her, but my leaving now does? OK, I guess that's fair.

The strength of the feeling told me Mani was close. *I can't let her into my world, can't let her mess up things with my friends.*

"I'm sorry. I can't explain right now. I am so sorry." I paused at the door. "Um…I shouldn't have kissed you." I took a deep breath. "I'm sorry."

She furrowed her eyebrows. "Maybe you need to apologize one more time." She smiled. Then I did. I felt her hand clutch my forearm—just when I was halfway through the open door. "And I'm not."

"Not what?"

"Sorry. I'm not sorry you kissed me."

Did she just say that? No time to ponder it: I ran out of the dorm, through the parking lot, to my truck, when the feeling intensified again. I turned the key, heard the roar of the engine, and pulled away. The feeling followed me, *tracking* me. *You're not funny, Mani. Stop toying with me.* Each new wave of sensation refueled my fury. Soon it was a genuine rage, which built up higher and higher, filling my lungs and pumping through my veins alongside my blood.

I drove, luring Mani away from Emma. *You're not going to ruin my life here on Earth.* But with each corner I turned, the feeling followed. I drove all the way to the outskirts of town, but still felt followed. When I finally felt far enough out of town, I stopped my truck. Closed my eyes to focus inward. She felt very close. I sighed, annoyance ripping me in shreds.

I opened my door and jumped out, slamming the door shut. Humidity gripped me. My t-shirt sealed itself against my sweaty skin. I walked away from my truck, into the black nothingness, and surveyed the area around me: left, right, back, front. Seeing nothing, no one, except for a pair of fields on either side of the long stretch of road. But still, I felt the presence. And with it I felt very, very annoyed.

I sighed. Turning back toward my truck, I heard a sound. Coming from behind, a scraping, kind of—no, more like feet dragging on the ground. I clenched my teeth – *a game of cat and mouse?* – slinking past my truck in that same direction.

Nope. Nothing there.

Was I now being used for Mani's personal amusement? *Enough is enough, Mani.* I felt a surge of heat, wondering if blood could actually boil. I then let everything out, yelling out into the night sky: "Enough. Show yourself or leave me be!"

Three days 'til the ritual. This is senseless, Mani. I refuse to let you follow me.

I waited for a reply, but only heard wind rustling through the trees. *I can play along, Mani.* I opened the driver's side door and slipped in. Looking around once more, I grabbed the keys I'd left in the ignition. Didn't look up. Didn't need to. I knew what I would see. I could *feel* it. With my eyes still glued to the ignition, I grabbed the door handle, leaped out, and spun around with rapid, alien speed, to face her at last, eye-to-eye. I pursed my lips, convinced anger would spew out of them if I dared open my mouth. Her smug expression seemed to touch me, lick me, shake my skin.

"Well, hello, Joshua," she mocked, her wine-colored lips folded upward into a grin. There it was: The same flirty look on her face that I'd fallen in love with years ago.

Funny. I felt annoyed this time, rather than aroused.

"What's the matter? Aren't you glad to see me?"

"Not especially."

"How rude. I'm glad to see you." She reached for my shirt collar.

I stepped back, avoiding her touch.

"Oh, it's to be like that, is it?"

I can fake not caring. I think. With her hair slicked back, her eyes looked bigger. I fought the attraction, remembering when she'd dumped me, how my insides had felt ripped out. That beauty was real, but it came at a steep price.

"I thought I made myself clear at your school. What do you *need*, Mani? The ritual's in three days. Have you heard something more about the guy in the article?"

"No. And do I really have to need something, Joshua? I can't just want to see you? I just can't accept that. We are the only two, the only two, of our kind on this great big planet. Not supporting each other is just plain stupid, not to mention heartless."

"I don't need or want your support." I turned toward my truck. "Why don't you go back to your little friends?"

"I have something to tell you." She paused.

I refused to respond. But I did turn back.

"Aren't you the least bit curious about what I've been doing in my free time?" She batted her eyelashes. I looked away, pretending not to notice.

"No, not really." I looked back. "But you're going to tell me anyway, aren't you?"

"You know me so well, my love." She followed my steps from a moment before, then stopped in front of me, her stare piercing deep into my eyes.

Can she see I still feel for her? I hope I'm hiding it. Keep – the – sides – of – your – mouth – down, Josh.

"I got a job in a restaurant on the other side of town, real fancy, big tips, business people."

Working as a waitress? What on Earth was she getting out of that? Where was that bold risk-taker I once knew? Back on Theos, Mani had worked as a scientific apprentice, just like me. I couldn't help myself: "You're working as a waitress?"

"Don't knock it. I've met all kinds of rich men. It's a hangout for very wealthy businessmen on the weekends." She licked her lips like an animal about to enjoy a meal. "I've done *very well.*"

"Mani, are you nuts? You're a minor. You're an alien. And you're getting involved with Earthlings? I bet you're even having relationships with them."

"Oh, I know the old teachings of staying clear, not mixing with the *unclean.* Ewww—just saying that makes me sick. No Theosian has ever lived here. Who are they to tell me—tell us—how to live?!" Her breath hit my face hard, along with her now screaming voice. She then took it down a notch and said, "You never give up old beliefs, do you?"

"There's good reason for them and you know it."

"Really? Well, according to *each* world, I'm both a minor and adult. The way I see it, it's my choice. In fact, so is *everything.*"

"You can't be both. We're on Earth, and Earth says we're minors. It isn't right, and you know it."

"*Do* you know it?" *She's certainly figured out how to slow this argument down, slow me down. And she knows how to get me to doubt myself. Gah!*

"What do you mean? Of course I know it."

"Oh, really? And what about your pretty little friend? What's her name? Emma?"

A mallet of pain split through the center of my brain. "What about her?"

She stared at me for some time before speaking again: "You love her," she whispered.

I looked away, wanting to do anything in the world but have this conversation.

"You know you do."

I kept my gaze away from hers. "I told her I can't have a relationship."

"Now, that's a lie. It's not that you can't have a relationship; you just can't have a relationship with *her*. Did you tell her that, Josh? Did you?"

The venom in her words slipped right down to my stomach, cultivating a subtle sickness. *You're a venomous snake, Mani. That's what you are.*

"No, I guess not. Instead, you just pretend like you don't love her, when you really do. You just keep spending every evening with her. I'm not stupid and neither are you. She'll see your back eventually, Josh. And then what?"

She laughed—simply laughed—at me!

I hate you, Mani. Hate you for being so right...

"And while we're on the subject, what about *your* age? Your *real* age. How dare you hold me to human standards, making yourself an exception? You're too young for her and you know that, too."

What can I say? Nothing. I can pretend I don't hear you. But—I got nothing.

She let out a loud sigh. "OK, if that's how you want to play it, we'll just wait and see what happens." She turned on her heels and began to swing her hips, stepping away from me.

"What's going to happen," I warned her, "is you're going back to your food service job and your little playschool and leaving me and my friends alone. Stop tracking me. Stop following me." My chest heaved. *Your beauty means nothing to me now.* "I don't want to see your face until Sunday. Do I make myself clear?"

She turned back to face me: "Sunday? For the ritual?"

"Oh, good. You figured it out." *Like she really forgot. Does she think I'm stupid?* "Now go."

"Oh, I'm gone, for now." Her vicious grin returned, chin pointed upward, face lit up by the moon. "You know we need each other."

"I didn't ask you to come to Earth with me. What you need is irrelevant to me. You had no right to come, no right." I turned to my truck. Hesitating as I opened the door, I began to look back, but immediately changed my mind. I slid in, slammed the door shut. My hand felt frozen around the key in the ignition.

"Chuchu tong," she said in our native tongue. *"Take care of yourself, friend."* Then, silence.

I looked into the rearview mirror. But I already knew. Gone. I couldn't feel her. I felt free...of her presence.

But still, that night, I couldn't sleep. I couldn't stop thinking about her.

19

CONFESSING

The aroma of damp leaves filled the air. How Earthlings took season changes for granted. But I rather enjoyed this unexpected perk. I especially enjoyed the crackle and crunch of dried leaves beneath my shoes during late fall. I watched cozy rituals like pumpkin-decorating, and I chuckled at the *alien* costumes on display in store windows. *Ha. Not quite, guys, but nice try.*

Normally on Fridays, my day off, I stayed away from the library, but not today. I had a mission. I found Cole mopping a tiled area on the second floor. He saw me approaching, but let on like he didn't. I stopped a few feet away, so as not to step on the area he'd already cleaned. "Hey, Cole. How's it going?"

"OK. You?" He kept on mopping.

"You up for supper at the café?" *I hope you remember our apology, or apology-like moment. 'Cause I certainly don't wanna do that again!*

"Huh?" Hmm, he'd never seemed weird about meeting me at the café before...

Oh—then something occurred to me, perhaps an ice-breaker. "I'm not asking you on a date." I smiled.

To my relief, he let out a snicker. "Yeah, I can do that."

"Cool." All of a sudden, I felt stupid standing there. "How's English going?"

"All right, a lot of work."

"Yeah, it is."

"You're smart. It's probably a breeze for you. Especially with Emma doing all your typing."

Talk about awkward. But why? "Yeah, it's cool not having to type." The silence that followed felt like some kind of endless limbo. Well, until I couldn't stand it anymore. "OK, see you at the café, say five?"

He nodded. I busted out of there, exhaling a weighted, awful breath, once I found myself safe outside the building.

A little after five o'clock, somewhat improbably even though we'd planned for it, I found myself sitting across from Cole. *Is he really going to keep talking about nothing? And keep shoving huge bites of that burger into his mouth?*

"Then State clobbered them 83-57. Blow out. They need a new coach."

Cutie pie waitress was off that day, so despite his significant limitations, he was managing to focus a little better on our "conversation." But I saw no sense in wasting time. *Maybe today, at some point, he'll notice I'm at the table. Come on, Josh. Get it over with. Dive in. I'm a brave Theosian. I'm a brave Theosian...*

I blurted it out. "I'm not gay, Cole."

He looked about, left and right. Then...straight down...uncaring, it seemed...at his food!

He's more worried about someone hearing, than about what I just said.

Then, finally: "OK."

It was all he said.

"That's all you have to say? I'm serious, and I shouldn't have let you think I was."

"Yeah," he said in between bites, "you shouldn't have." No anger, though.

Or at least, I didn't hear anger. His voice sounded monotone. *What happened to him? He lost his soul?!*

"It was all about Emma. I didn't want to have to explain why I was avoiding her."

Cole picked up his drink, took a little sip. Suddenly, his face contorted. "Do you think I'm stupid?" He slammed his glass onto the table. Soda leaped upward then landed back in the glass.

What the...? Not feeling quite so hungry anymore, I pushed my plate forward. "So, I guess you figured out that I like her, too?"

"Yeah, I figured as much the day *I told you I liked her.* You know, when you just about bit my head off, or whatever you were thinking about doing to me."

I may not have known much, but I knew *he* didn't *want* to know what I really felt like doing that day. "Sorry about that."

"Forget it." He shoved the last of his burger into his mouth, which had ketchup oozing out of its corners.

What's he thinking? What's he mean by that? How can I forget this?

"I'm backing off. Bro code, you know."

"What?"

"Bro code?" His stare confirmed I was obviously missing something.

"Oh, bro code, right." *Note to self: Look up the term bro code.* "I wish my life wasn't so—complicated."

"Complicated? Well, if anything's complicated, it's girls."

Huh? Anyway, looks like we're good. Close one.

"Yeah." No sooner than I'd finished talking, that *feeling*, followed by an instant stomachache, rushed back into my body. *Not her again. I thought I made myself clear yesterday.* This crap had to stop. I looked up to see Mani flounce up to our table, just as we stood to leave.

She obviously meant to impress with her outfit. Skin-tight, dark blue dress, exposing enough leg to entice any male who wasn't legally blind (or, you know, gay). Make-up heavy, hair up, she was trying to look older, too, and certainly succeeding. *Ouch. Cole doesn't stand a chance.* Mani leaned over, exposing some cleavage. *Don't look, Josh. Don't look.*

"Josh, so good to see you," she said, smiling widely.

"Josh, who's this?" Cole wasted no time.

At that moment, I knew. The game just changed—for the worse.

20

INTRODUCING

"Cole...this is Mani," I said reluctantly. "She's...an old friend."

Mani stood fully upright.

"Good to meet you," Cole pulled out a chair and flashed an extra-wide smile.

"Hello." My stomach churned. Every bat of her eyelashes made it churn all the more.

"So, you and Josh are old friends, huh? From high school?"

I stared at her. *Careful what you say, Mani...*

"High school? Yes, high school. We were lab partners."

"Chemistry," I said quickly. "We were...lab partners...in Chemistry class."

She flashed a grin.

"Ah, I see. Lucky guys share petri dishes with lab partners like you..."

Ugh, really, Cole? Is that the best you can do?

"I haven't seen you on campus, Mani." Cole's smile remained so wide I could iron my shirt on it.

"No, I don't go here. I...work...at a diner on the other side of town. I work later today, actually."

OK, that's enough out of you, Mani. "Mani," I said. "I'll walk you out." I grabbed her arm; she rose with my pull. Before I could maneuver her through the tables, Cole quickly stepped forward, so as not to miss another second of flirting (or whatever it was he was attempting).

"I hope to see you again." Cole couldn't help but lean in toward Mani as he said this.

"So do I."

Before I actually hurled, I stepped in between their two sets of playful eyes and grabbed her arm, leading her out the door and away from the cafe.

She came willingly for a while, then yanked free and strutted in front of me. She then remained silent 'til we ended up on the sidewalk across the street from the café.

I glared, annoyed.

She glared back. "How dare you?"

"Just what do you think *you're* doing?"

"Your friend is ca-yute." She aimed her gaze back toward the café doors.

"I told you to stay away."

"Oh, yeah, um…about that. I was going to, really I was, but…I decided it might be more fun to meet your friends." She sounded chipper. She snapped her gum.

"And you actually think I wanted you to meet them?"

"Why not?" Now she crossed her arms over her chest – a defensive posture. Ready for a fight.

"You're not exactly good at keeping your mouth shut, and if you haven't noticed, I don't intend on explaining where I come from anytime soon."

"I won't tell anyone."

Yeah, like I trust you. Her face fell.

Is she going to CRY? "Seriously?"

"Yes, seriously." She dabbed the tears under her eyes. "If you let me in your little circle of friends, then I promise, I will keep your...I mean our...secret, a secret."

"Blackmail won't work. And besides, I already told Emma you and I used to be together."

"Did you now?"

"Look, I don't want her being friends with my ex." I started to leave, but she grabbed my forearm.

"I won't be a problem. I won't say anything...not about you and me...not about Theos...not about anything."

Naturally, this really was the farthest thing from a good idea, but if I didn't give in, the potential consequences were dire. Among all the other things that Mani was, I knew she certainly was *not* a good loser. "Mani: If you cause any problems, so help me—"

"Don't worry. I won't." She smiled at me, the very essence of wickedness.

"They can't know you're in high school."

"Fine. As far as they're concerned, I'm just a waitress, OK?"

You're playing with fire, Josh. But she stirred something in me—something I didn't want stirred. *I love Emma. Yeah, that's right.*

Just concentrate on Emma.

The next day brought more of the same: time with Emma, studying in my dorm room. Only this time, *she* looked like the distracted one. When we finished one of her essays, there was zero reaction from her. *Come on: Ask questions, or worry. Something!*

"What's wrong?"

"Nothing."

Eyes down. Voice higher. She's lying!

She sighed. Then: "It's us," she whispered. "You know, what's going on...with you and me? I hate not knowing even if there *is* a you and me."

Instinctively, I gathered up her books and binders into a neat pile. "I'm not sure, either." I knew my answer wouldn't help, but it was the truth. "I keep thinking, trying to work things out in my head."

"I'm sorry." Her eyes dropped again. "I'm trying to be patient...to handle the *friend* thing." Her weight shifted back and forth from one leg to the other, restless. No tears dropped from her eyes...at least not yet.

The last thing I ever want to do is hurt her...

Her gaze finally lifted. She looked into my eyes.

I studied her face, when I felt her hand touch my waist. Time stopped. Before I could think, our lips were enmeshed. I couldn't resist her taste, her warmth. Maybe she pulled, maybe I lost balance – either way, I found myself plummeting down onto the couch, on top of her. Uncontrollably, I pressed my body onto hers. Felt that familiar electric current, this time stronger than ever.

I heard us both breathing hard. *It's hotter in here.* I tried to think of something else—where are we again?

But, my body didn't care where – not what room, what building, what city...

Slam. Reality hit hard. *Control yourself. Now!* I forced myself to pull back, and sit up. Both of us gasped for air.

"What's wrong?" she asked, pushing her curls away from her eyes.

"Emma," I panted. "We can't."

"Why not? Did I do something wrong?"

"No, of course not." I wiped my lips dry with my sleeve. "You're amazing. But you can't just...trust me...without knowing me. You have no idea what you're getting yourself into."

"What? You're a murderer, some kind of criminal—?"

"Of course not." I laughed.

"Then, no worries." She pulled me back down on top of her and, for a second, I considered giving in. I felt like I'd just drank an entire pack of klendduk. Theosian alcohol, I guess one could call it. Only ours didn't come with a horrible case of hurling welskies the morning after, like here on Earth.

Our lips entangled, our hands explored – everywhere, hers under my shirt and over my back, my sure to be *brightly glowing* back. I pulled away. *She can't see that.*

We both sat up again, breathing heavily. I reached out to smooth her hair. Tugged at the bottom of my shirt. Picked up a pillow we'd knocked onto the carpet.

Did anything but look into her eyes.

21

STRUGGLING

What's wrong with me? Every guy on campus would go for it. And the second time, no less! She's going to think I am *gay. This is getting worse, much worse.* "You have to just trust me. We have to stop."

"Why?"

I cringed, outside and in. Didn't have an answer.

"Don't think I don't want to. I really, really want to be with you. We just have to wait."

"You're acting like there's something wrong with you, but I'm fairly sure everything's in working order." She grinned. Devilish. Trying to keep the mood upbeat.

I smiled. *Can't believe she just said that.* "Yes, everything's…uh…working. Waiting…is just the right thing."

She breathed in and out again, studying my face. *I wish I could read faces as well as Earthlings.*

"OK, I'm not sure why, but…I'll go along with this *waiting is the right thing* plan. But I do wish I could know why."

Sensing a change in the room, I joked: "Girls get to decide when the time is right. Why can't a guy?"

"Because it's just plain weird. That's why." Poof! Just like that, we were good again. *Phew.*

"No one has ever trusted me like that, Emma."

"Well, someone does now."

Sunday. Short work day. Emma and my schedules overlap by one hour. But this Sunday called for something else. One day a year, Mani and I had to complete the ritual in order to continue to live within Earth's atmosphere.

That day...was today.

How did my parents miss this in their research? They knew everything about Earth. They understood every type of gas, liquid, chemical, plant, animal, and micro-organism. Why didn't they foresee the need for the ritual? Unless they left it out for some purpose. But why?

By the time Emma arrived at the library for her short shift, I'd repeatedly played and replayed the night before in my head. I winked. She winked. I smiled. She smiled. I stared at the clock, wanting it to move faster. *Just want to get the ritual over. But what lie will I tell Emma about not hanging with her tonight?*

"Ugh," I said, clutching my stomach with both hands. "I really don't feel so good." *Are both hands too much?* I lowered one.

"Really? Maybe it's the flu."

"Maybe, but I'm thinking you better not come over tonight."

"Oh, really?" She made pouty lips. "Well, OK. Maybe I'll see you Monday?"

"Maybe, I'll have to see how I feel."

We walked to her car. *Does she expect a kiss? Do we do that anymore?*

"I shouldn't kiss you. Don't wanna make you sick, too." *What's going on? Why am I acting so weird?*

I drove straight to the outskirts of town. Guilt ate away at me; I almost *did* feel sick. The black sky enveloped the fields on either side of the road, yet dim streetlights interrupted the blackness. *Quiet and desolate, exactly what we need...*

I sensed her the second she came close. And I stayed in my truck, knowing exactly where she was. I didn't even have to look up.

"Ready?" I asked.

"Hello to you, too, Josh."

My stare toward her wasn't openly hostile, but was far from neighborly. I opened the door and stepped out. "Let's get this over with."

"Always in such a hurry. You know, if you weren't such a stubborn person, you might realize how lucky you are that you have another Theosian around, so you *can* do the ritual in order to survive on your blessed, little planet."

"You came along uninvited. You live like a high school teen. You live irresponsibly amongst the humans, and now you've pushed yourself into my group of friends and you want me to exchange pleasantries? Like I said, let's just get this over with."

"OK, OK." She stepped up to face me, taking the traditional ritual pose. But not without first sticking out her tongue. I ignored her.

I closed my eyes, which was not exactly necessary, but I wanted to. We stood face to face, a foot apart. My sensing ability hit a point of overload. Energy began to build between us. Quickly, I felt warmer and warmer.

When the warmth reached a certain level, we each instinctively stepped forward, narrowing the small gap.

As we raised our hands above our heads, the energy formed a complete oval. Then our arms straightened and our fingers intertwined. A surge, an electrical current, shot through me. I could tell by her shudder, she felt it, too. I didn't need to open my eyes to know the golden aura now encased both our bodies. It looked similar in color to the love glow that emanates from our Theosian backs. But this glow held the energy necessary for our bodies to survive on Earth.

I remembered sitting through our Prehistorical Survival class, back on Theos. It was one of those classes you never think you'll need in real life. Anyway, it was a good thing I'd taken it, or Mani and I would be dust by now.

The energy spurred a burst of movement. We writhed back and forth, left to right, then left again. If overheard, our moaning would most likely be misinterpreted. But to us, it was all just part of the process.

After 20 minutes, the energy died down. The ritual was coming to an end, finally, for another whole year. I could feel the energy around us replenished by the ritual. But still, I wished we didn't need to do this. Maybe I could figure out some other way to go about it—a way that didn't involve *her*.

Our hands fell to our sides. My eyes fluttered open. Standing so close felt weird. But Mani grinned. I stepped back away from her, then wasted no time in walking toward my truck door.

"Well, it was really nice seeing you again. You take care now."

Nothing like sarcasm to win me back. Sigh.

"Just don't do or say something stupid around my friends." As before, I didn't even look at her. I started my engine and drove off. *She's like a freakin' loaded bomb. And now she knows Cole. I hope this doesn't get any worse. But what do I expect? It's Mani.*

22

GUILTING

I dragged myself through morning classes, guilt burning a hole in my stomach. *I actually lied to Emma...to be with Mani. That damn ritual. What's the point of surviving when you feel like this?*

Cole knew I had class 'til 6, so he showed up at my dorm room a little after. Stemmy was *studying* with his girlfriend in our room, so Cole and I went into the lounge to watch some Monday night football on the television. Several other guys slouched in cushy chairs around the TV. I heard cans popping open and smelled a strange mixture of buttered popcorn and stinky socks.

During a commercial, I caught Cole looking my way, grinning.

"What?"

"You know very well what."

Um, nope...I really didn't.

"Huh?" *This is one alien who can't read minds.*

"Don't worry, I'm not expecting details."

"Whatever kind of details you're referring to, I don't think I *would* give them to you, judging by the look on your face."

"Nah, I'm just teasing. I'm happy for you, man."

"Happy for me? Happy for me about what?"

"You and Emma, man." He cracked open his second pop, threw back a swig. "You think I can't tell, the way you two were looking at each other in the library yesterday?"

I just stared. I hadn't even seen him in the library the day before. How did *he* see us?

"My boss had me checking out the surveillance cameras. You two were downright cute." He shoved me. Instinctively, I shoved back.

"Now, that's a little creepy, to think you were eavesdropping on people all over the library."

"First of all, if they don't want people to see them, they shouldn't do anything funky in the library. Secondly, yeah, it was creepy, but really kind of creepy cool." He laughed.

I looked back at the TV. I guess it didn't matter. *So what? He saw Emma and me looking at each other. No biggie.*

The game was a blow-out. Afterward, Cole decided to head back to his dorm. I figured Stemmy must be done *studying* by now.

As Cole left the lounge, he spun back around:

"Hey, by the way, your old friend, Mani, she's a real doll." Before I could come up with a response, he let out a "Yowza," and left the room.

Yep, there it was. This was gonna be really, really bad.

23

EMMA

Tuesday morning at the library. *Not as stressful as they used to be.* Josh's assigned work took him to the third floor most of the time, which meant we had to work less at hiding our flirty glances. Besides, I liked having more time for girl talk with Kaylee. Well, kind of...

"Tell me more, tell me more: You a*ctually* pulled him down on the couch? Then what happened?"

The truth was, Kaylee's need for details made me feel really uncomfortable. I mean, I was too embarrassed to ask her for her *own* details. Not that I had to ask; she told me everything. "Well," I said, "we kissed, and kissed, and kissed..." Our giggles were shushed by a couple of other girls, studying nearby, so we walked to the corner of the floor, where I resumed: "And then, he stopped...again."

"What the heck is going on with him?"

"I don't know. And then he said the weirdest thing. He said 'Trust me, waiting is the right thing to do.'"

"Waiting is the right thing to do? That is weird. Well, sounds like he thinks it'll happen in the future, right?"

"I can't figure him out, Kaylee." I stood there, lost in thought for what must have been forever. I kept replaying that scene from the couch in my head. A sudden burst of chatter from some people behind me in the stairwell made my shoulders jump. I looked around for Kaylee, but she was nowhere in sight. The strange thing was, I didn't remember her leaving, and as I looked around, I couldn't see a soul. *Oh, no. It's closing time!*

I hurried to the break room and grabbed my purse and lunch bag from my locker. Then I headed out the front doors, just a moment before the security guard jangled his keys to lock it.

Destination: Josh's dorm. *Maybe I can figure out what's going on with him. Hopefully Stemmy's downstairs with his girlfriend...*

24

FUMING

Tuesday. Third floor library. No Emma. Torture. *I miss seeing her.* I carried a book downstairs, pretending it belonged on the second floor, and caught sight of Kaylee and Emma talking and giggling together. *What I wouldn't give to hear that conversation. Er, maybe I don't want to know.* I went back upstairs to be lonely working on my own.

By quitting time, I raced back down the steps, eager to see Emma. But: No Emma. No Kaylee. *No need to worry. We have a standing study date tonight. I'll just go back to my room to get ready for that.*

Cool-looking shirt? Check. Her favorite snacks? Got 'em. And Stemmy had agreed to hang out in Sam's room for the night. *Can I control myself, being alone with her? Can I make good on my plan to wait? I have to...*

The much-anticipated knock finally came.

She's here. Play it cool, Josh. I swung the door open.

"Hey, I thought tonight we could--" I stopped mid-sentence. My smile fell. My stomach sank and churned at the same time. I felt my fists clench. I stood there frozen in the open doorway, staring at Mani, who snickered, in an apparent state of total enjoyment.

"Sorry to disappoint you. Were you expecting someone else?"

I turned away from the door, leaving it wide open. "Funny. What now?"

She flounced into the room behind me.

"You really know how to make an old friend feel welcome," she chided.

I turned back. "Mani, this isn't a good time."

"Yeah, I should have sent you a text." She dug around in her handbag, pulling out a cell phone. "These things are so ridiculous, so archaic."

"Mani, what do you expect them to do? It's not as if they have built-in tracking devices like we do." Then something very peculiar occurred to me: "Hey, I didn't know it was you at the door." *I didn't sense her, not at all. How did she do that?*

"You really didn't?"

"No, I thought it was Emma." I walked to the door, which was still hanging open, then stuck my head out and looked left and right. No Emma. I closed it and turned back around.

"Well, anyway." She strolled deeper into my room, positioning herself in front of the window. The stream of light from the lamp post outside created a sleek silhouette. "I was wondering if Cole had anything to say about me."

"Mani, you should leave him alone."

"It's not your place to talk, baby."

"Honestly, Mani, I don't want you to end up with the same problem I have."

"Yeah, um, you didn't look like a guy with a problem a minute ago, when you opened that door."

I averted my gaze. "It's more of a problem than you think."

"Yeah, yeah, yeah. Blah, blah, blah."

"Look, I don't have time for this right now." I walked back to the door, pulling it open wide, welcoming her to leave.

And so she swaggered back toward the door, swinging her hips (which were, by the way, tightly wrapped in a mini-skirt). "OK, I'm going." She hesitated, then leaned in close to me and spoke very softly, breathing on my face: "I remember when you used to look at me that way, like you did when you opened the door."

"That was a long time ago."

"Not that long ago, as I remember it."

As I parted my lips to tell her once more to leave, Emma popped up in the doorway.

Mani, still standing provocatively close to me, didn't move an inch.

I decided to take a step back. *Oh, it's too freakin' late, now. Should have got her out sooner, Josh....*

"Emma. Hi." I pushed Mani aside to stand directly facing Emma. My stomach felt like it was full of something toxic. Maybe what humans had in theirs – acid. "Um...Mani was just leaving." I turned back to Mani. "I'll tell Cole you said hi."

"Yeah, I'll see ya around." Mani swung her mini-skirt out of the room.

I shut the door and turned to Emma, hoping to somehow salvage the moment. But I was now in deep trouble with her for absolutely nothing, thanks to Mani.

Emma stayed silent. Her feelings were written on her face, as the humans say. I couldn't read expressions, but even I knew I was in big, big trouble. She dropped her jacket and purse, turned directly to me. She didn't yell, but her words cut me just the same.

"You have a choice to make, right now. You either tell me everything or we're done, completely done, no questions, no exceptions. You choose...*right now*."

25

LOSING

It felt like everything good in my life was flipping upside-down. I stepped toward Emma, ready to at least attempt to reassure her, but she raised her hand, keeping distance between us. Worse than that, she didn't look at me. She looked away.

"Emma," I pleaded gently. "Slow down."

"Make...the...choice." No room for discussion, apparently. No leeway. She talked not to me, but to the floor.

"Can we please talk about it?" *I want to hold you. Let me explain.* I took one step forward. She took two steps back.

"There's nothing to talk about, except your choice."

"I'll explain everything."

She looked up at me.

Good. Progress. "Just give me a little time--"

Nope. Again, she looked away.

"What? You seem to have plenty of time for *her.* You think I'm dumb? You think I haven't figured out she's your ex?"

Yelling. Emma never yells. Worse than I thought...

"I didn't ask her to come here. I didn't want her here. I told her to stay away." My words exploded from my lips like bullets, with Emma as their target.

"There's nothing between us. We are nothing but friends."

"Oh, really? When we were *just friends,* you didn't stand that close to me, ever."

"You're right. And I should have told you she lived here. But, I didn't invite her here. I wanted her to leave. I promise, Emma." *I can't lose you.* "She stood close to *me.* I opened the door and told her to leave."

"And you *chose* not to back away from her. Why?"

Even I didn't know the answer to that one. What could I say? Maybe she was right. *Maybe I still feel...something for Mani. If so, I hate it. Emma's perfection. And now I'm losing her. I'd do anything for her! Wish I knew what I could do.*

"Right. I have my answer. An unspoken, loud and clear, ridiculous, freaking stupid answer." She grabbed her purse and jacket, tears running down her cheeks.

I ran after her, begging. "Emma. Emma, please. It's you I want."

She didn't turn around. She didn't stop. Just kept walking.

Why? What is wrong with me? Why don't I have the answer this time either?

26

SCREAMING

It's hard to say where the next couple of hours went. Everything, *everything* seemed a blur. I felt encapsulated in some thick, impenetrable fog. Parts of my body – my hands, my feet – felt rubbery, as if they weren't real in some way. Next thing I knew, I was running, not remembering the choice to start doing so. Moreover, I looked down to see sweats, a t-shirt, and a jacket. When had I changed my clothes?

And not just running, but running in the rain. *I must be losing my mind. No Emma. No sanity.* I saw my body, too, soaking wet. *I just don't care.* My breath shot out of my mouth in white bursts while my skin remained only vaguely aware of the coldness.

Eventually, sweat and raindrops mixed together on my skin. But as the rain slowed to a drizzly stop, sweat took its place. *I'm burning up.* I unzipped my jacket and threw it to the ground, but kept on running. I felt pain, but not in my muscles, not physical pain in my body. *I can understand that. I can handle that. But this unbearable emotion? Nope, can't take it.*

As my emotions swelled, my feet powered faster, pounding the ground. Sweat poured down my face, dripped from my hands. I ripped off my t-shirt, throwing it behind me. My feet, continually pounding the pavement. I stopped, looking back at the glow of the city lights. Stood there, surrounded again by miles of fields. The remoteness freed me. I slowed my pace until I was walking...and then barely putting one foot in front of the other. I turned my head from side to side, scanning the entire area. *What are you looking for? Your sanity?*

Suddenly, all the heavy emotions rushed through my body, like a mad fire. Wind, swirling and twisting, beat against my body. I looked to the sky as a beastly scream left my throat, speeding in an upward direction. My body weakened. Heart, slashed. Exhausted, I collapsed to my knees in a heap, my back hunched over, taste of dirt in my mouth. Then air filled my lungs and a throaty shrill escaped my mouth. *Is that coming from me?* It went on, and on, 'til finally...just a limp and bubbly gurgle.

27

RELINQUISHING

My body heaved for air, palms scraping the cold, hard ground beneath me. I remained hunched over. The swirling wind quieted. I struggled to catch my breath, aware of that *feeling* again. *Not again.* I raised my head, glanced side to side.

At that moment, I heard a sound, like someone shifting their weight, then dragging their shoes across dirt-covered ground. Instinctively defensive, I jumped to my feet and spun around to confront my aggressor, knees bent, body crouched.

My rival looked ready, in fighting stance. We stared, two animals prepared to pounce. Mani lifted her chin and began to speak, her voice raspy and loud:

"Look closely at me, Josh."

"I see you clearly, Mani."

"Yes, but do you *really* see?"

You have my attention.

"As I have said before, here we are, alone on this planet, together. Forget why. Why doesn't matter. You're in pain. I'm in pain. Only I can really understand the pain you feel, Josh. I understand you."

"You caused me this pain."

"Did I? Did I, really?"

I understood. *It's my fault. I can blame myself.* I *knew* better than to let myself fall for an Earthling. Not to mention one of age.

I relaxed my stance. She did the same.

She walked a few steps forward, melting against me, breathing on my face.

Once again, I didn't move away. *I remember what drew me to you. You're beautiful. And you do understand. No one understands me like you do. I need someone to understand me.*

As we drew closer to each other, Emma's face flickered in my mind. *I love her. But I can't be with her.* I wrapped my arms around her. *You're so warm.* Pulled her close to me. Remained lost in the pleasure of the glow only Theosians could produce. *This…is… awesome. Mani's the one I need.*

PART THREE

Do we really belong...anywhere?

28

BELONGING

I called in sick the next day, which was fitting since I *did* feel sick. At least, my mind felt sick. *Wish it had a delete button. Why? Why get back with Mani? And why does it feel good? It shouldn't. I thought I loved Emma.*

My cell rang throughout the day. I didn't have to look. I knew. Cole. Emma wouldn't be calling. Not anymore.

Why not Mani? She's fun. She's Theosian. It's just easier that way, right?

I completely avoided Emma and Cole. It wasn't much of a challenge, since I could tell they were both avoiding me, too. *Whatever, I don't have to talk to them. I don't have to talk to anybody, if I don't want to.*

I finally went back to work on Thursday. Emma was working, too, but I paid no attention, just did my job. At quitting time, I grabbed my belongings and bolted to the elevator, anxious to see Mani. As the door opened and some riders filed out, I boarded and turned to see Emma stepping on as well. Of course we'd be the only two on it. *Just my luck. Awk-ward.*

The ride down felt like 10 stories instead of two. We stood in total silence, unless you count the elevator engine. I held back, allowing her to step off first, walking slowly a few steps behind her. *Don't look down. Don't breathe. Don't do anything.*

In the parking lot, so empty and quiet, I called her name. *What are you doing, Josh? Shut your mouth, now.*

Her footsteps stopped. She turned and faced me, eye to eye.

"How are you?" *If only I could stop myself...*

"I'm good." Her face, the essence of neutrality. "You?"

"Good." Awkward. Silence.

"Good. I guess we're both...good then." She turned to continue toward her car.

"Emma?"

She spoke to me. I can't believe it. She actually spoke to me. Does she forgive me? It can't be. What does this mean?

She turned back around.

I drew a blank. Nothing passed through my lips. I *did* want to say something. But, no words seemed like the right ones. After realizing what an idiot I had become, I wrapped it up. "Take care, that's all. Just...take care."

Her lips turned up at the corners. A smile!

Or...maybe I'd imagined it? Humans called this wishful thinking.

In any case, she didn't speak.

I can accept that. At least we stayed pleasant. Weird, but pleasant. That's something. Isn't it?

That night, Mani snuggled against me on my dorm room couch. Stemmy? Out once again. She read her fashion magazine while I enjoyed soaking up the sight of the wall. *I guess I should be studying or something.* I reached forward and grabbed a textbook.

"What's up, Josh?"

"Oh, nothing really." I stared at the textbook, or past it, really.

She re-positioned her head, looking straight into my face.

"Oh, it's just...well...I...saw Emma today." I flipped the textbook around in my hands, in a crazed kind of circular motion.

"And?"

"Nothing, really. We just said hi. It was... awkward."

"So, what about it?" She wasn't blinking, just looking at me. Through me. "You were just wasting your time with her, anyways."

"Why the attitude?" Hot prickles erupted on the back of my neck.

"No attitude. I just don't get why you waste your time talking to her."

"Waste my time?"

"Don't be so sensitive, Josha."

"Joshua, remember?"

"Whatever. She doesn't matter. Don't waste your time."

"I think you're jealous."

"Jealous?" Her magazine slapped down against the floor. She had thrown it! "When you look like this, no one else matters."

I stood up and stared down at her. *What is she saying?* "No one else matters? Don't waste my time? You know, your face is pretty, but your selfishness is ugly, very ugly."

"I've done well for myself." Her grin – so uncaring, so completely uncaring. "It got you, didn't it?"

"What?"

"What, you think it was just fate? I knew Emma was coming over. I got here first. And I knew you jogged out to that field."

"You set me up and I fell right into it." I leaned in and over her, just a bit. "You bitch!"

"Give me a break," she said, scooping up her magazine and resuming her reading.

"I hate this part of you. You're so cold. Get out." *I'm such a fool. Liking both of them...*

"Shut up."

I walked to the door and held it open, just as I had two nights before. But this time, I would finish it right. "You are a total bitch."

She stared at me, looking confused, almost innocent, a sickening sense of self-righteousness in her eyes. She eventually stood up and strutted over, mocking me.

"And you love me anyways." Her smile, sickening. "You need me. You'll see. Without me, you're completely alone. The ritual won't be enough. She doesn't know you. She can't understand you. You…need…me."

"I'd rather die."

"Careful what you wish for."

I slammed the door and went to bed, alone.

29

FALLING

*I'm such an idiot. Alone on Theos. Alone on Earth.
I'm sick—so sick—of ending up alone all the time.
Mani worked me like a puppet. Made me lose Emma.
And I'll never want Mani after this. Ever.*

I forced myself to go to the library after class. My
stomach grumbled, but I couldn't eat. No appetite. And
nothing tasted right anyway. Even the fall leaves
seemed to have lost their color. The sun, instead of
giving warmth, simply hurt my eyes. I enjoyed
nothing.

After work, I took the stairs. *Not getting in that
elevator again.* On the second floor, I caught a glimpse
of Cole and Emma sitting in the break room, through
the glass in the door behind the circulation desk. I
ducked behind some bookshelves to watch them.

Suddenly, my stomach grumbled so loud that no
less than three different people turned and stared.
"Sorry," I mouthed. I pulled a chocolate bar from my
hoodie pocket, ripped it open as silently as possible,
and bit off a chunk. I looked up to see the same three
people, still staring at me. "What? I'm eating. OK?" I
mouthed again.

I peeked through shelves. Cole was still sitting
across from Emma. I saw their mouths moving. *Wish I
could read lips...*

Cole stood up and leaned toward Emma, lifting her chin with his hand.

What the hell was he gonna do? Don't kiss her.

He kissed her cheek.

I jumped back to hide myself completely as he walked out through the door and down the stairs to leave.

They are together. Where does that leave me? I can't be Cole's friend and Emma's ex. I can't. This chocolate's going to come back up. How dare Cole. And how could she *move on already?*

The break room door opened. Emma walked through, head down. I attempted to look through books, only catching short, disjointed glimpses of her. Not wanting to look anymore, I closed my eyes and walked to the corner to collapse into a stuffed chair. After feeling around for what was left of the candy bar in my pocket, I pulled it out and dropped it in the trash can. *Trash. Just like whatever me and Emma had.*

Seconds later, I felt my cell phone vibrate. *Better not be Cole. He's the last person I want to talk to. The first person I'd like to punch, but the last I want to talk to.* My body tingled and tightened as I read the contact name: *Emma.* I read the text five times:

I want to know who you really are. Will you tell me your secrets?

She's giving me a second chance? But...what about Cole? What I just saw? I didn't care. I typed back: *Yes.*

How? When?

Any time you say.

ASAP.

Tonight? My dorm?

Her response came almost instantly:*I'll be there.*

What just happened? My hands trembled. *What about her and Cole? Why give me another chance?* I grabbed my backpack and jumped to my feet. Three words escaped my mouth. "A second chance."

More library patrons turned their heads and shushed me.

Time passed very quickly, too quick. Now I understood what humans mean when they say time drags when you want it to hurry and hurries when you are dreading the future. I waited on the couch in my dorm. After she finally arrived, we did the same thing as before: sat on the couch in silence. Waiting made no difference. I figured I might as well get this over with.

"My name is Josha. Josha Hummak." I stared at her, trying to read her face. Nothing. "That's my given name. I changed it to Joshua Denaugh."

"OK." She obviously (rightfully!) expected more.

"It's so hard to explain. I have spent days trying to figure out the words to explain to you." *You're blowing your final chance. Do it now.* "Come, let me show you something."

She nodded. We stood and I took her hand, leading her over to the window. I closed the curtains and after turning down the lights, I stared directly into her eyes.

"You have to trust me." *Who's the one with the trust issues here?* "Don't be afraid of me."

She remained still and silent, standing facing me. I looked down and took her hand in mine, raised it to my mouth to softly kiss her silky skin. She smiled. She wanted to know the truth, right? *Here it goes...*

"Lift up my shirt and look at my back," I instructed. My directives rendered her frozen, it seemed. I leaned in close to her and whispered into her ear: "Lift up my shirt and look into the glass frame behind me on the wall. You wanted to know the truth. You deserve the truth, Emma. And you better hurry before I lose my nerve."

So she raised her hands and grabbed the bottom of my dark t-shirt, never taking her eyes off mine until I looked away. Then her eyes moved away and toward Stemmy's framed picture of one of his favorite professional athletes. Her eyes widened as her lower lip dropped, along with her jaw, opening her mouth slightly. My stomach churned.

I lifted my hands and placed them onto her arms, just below each shoulder. Her eyes were glued to the reflection, mesmerized it seemed. But she spoke.

30

TRUSTING

"It's…it's beautiful. What is it?"

"It means…It means I feel…love."

Questions darted from her eyes. "So, you feel love…right now? For me?"

What's she thinking? Does she believe me? I answered with a nod.

"Can I touch it?"

"Sure. You've…touched it before. You just didn't know it."

She slid her fingers over my back, watching the reflection. When she seemed adjusted (to the extent that such was possible) to this bit of knowledge, I led her to the couch.

"I'm different," I whispered.

She laughed. "Just a little. Is there… more?"

I nodded. Turned the lights up. "Don't be afraid. But watch." I took her hand, inhaling deeply and slowly. I focused…vanishing.

She gasped suddenly, so I reappeared, squeezing her hand.

"What the…?"

"I know." I wrapped my arm around her shoulder. "It's OK. I'm here. I'm still…me."

Her hands touched my chest gently, as if making sure I was real.

"Let's just sit here for a minute," I said.

"I'm OK. I'm OK." She seemed to be trying to convince herself more than me. "What else can you do?"

"Well, I can *feel* the presence of particular beings." That was it. I had officially entered very dangerous territory.

"What beings? Me?"

"No."

"Then who?"

"Others...like me."

"There are others like you? What do you mean?" Her voice quivered. Her hands shook. I'd expected this. But, at least she wasn't running away. Not yet.

"Yes."

Silence. She continued shaking.

I realized my hands shook, too. "What are you thinking?" Our entire conversation, whispers.

Her voice came out almost inaudible, barely a whisper, like a wisp of breath. "You...aren't from this world." She didn't say it as a question. It sounded more like a statement. Then she added, "I don't know what to think. But I'm not afraid of you. I love you."

"There's no reason to be afraid. Really...I promise...I love you, too."

I can't remember how many pots of coffee we ended up drinking after that. I just knew it was a lot...

"So, once a year you and Mani have to perform a *ritual*?"

"Yeah. It's really more of a survival treatment. If we don't, the atmosphere will make us weak and sick. I

143

put together some scientific processes I learned back on Theos, when we both started to show signs of atmospheric breakdown."

"When will it be time again?"

"We just did it a few days ago, so not for almost a year."

She took yet another sip of coffee. "So, how do you do it?"

"We stand, facing each other, raise and connect hands. The energy between us multiplies. There's a bright glow and that's about all."

She flashed me a grin. "What else is coming? Mars? Martians?"

Laughter spilled out of my mouth. Despite her smile, she failed to see the humor, so I got serious again. "OK. Fair question, I guess."

"Yeah, so what about it?"

"Myth," I said. "There's no life on Mars. Your government isn't lying about that." *Uh, oh, pace yourself, buddy...*

"So, why haven't I ever heard of Theos?"

"NASA hasn't developed a spacecraft sophisticated enough to reach Theos, or our neighboring planets." I rose to reach for the box of doughnuts, then set them on the coffee table.

"Other...planets?"

"Hey, how about we break for now," I suggested. "I'll tell you more later, all right?"

"All right. We should talk about us."

How can female Earthlings think of so much to ask and to say? What's coming next? I'm exhausted.

"Never mind that. I know you're with Cole," I said looking away. "I screwed up. I know it."

When she didn't answer...I knew. I heard her take a deep breath. Then silence. Then another big breath. *All bad signs.*

"Friends?" she asked.

"Yes. I'm lucky you're even willing to go that far. And I can keep hoping you change your mind, right?"

She smiled, then yawned and rubbed her eyes. "I'm exhausted. I need to go back to my dorm and shower and get some sleep."

Tomorrow, she'll wake up and decide I'm a freak. Way to go, Josh. You finally took a chance at being yourself. And what do you get? Friends. Just friends with Emma.

At the door, she turned. "Josh, it means a lot to me, you know, telling me the truth. But, I just don't know what to think of it. I mean...my brain's on overload."

"I wanted to tell you the truth sooner. But, I was..."

"Scared? Yeah, I can see why. And to think I bothered you with being worried about my little sis and her choice in boyfriends."

"What's wrong with that? It's important."

"Yeah, right." She rolled her eyes.

"*More* important as far as I'm concerned."

We hugged. She left. My...*friend.*

31

REALIZING

Emma still came by my dorm, just not as often as she had prior. *Friends, now.* More importantly, our bodies never touched, she never once mentioned Cole, and for my part, I stayed away from the two of them at the library.

Every day, though, she thought of new questions to ask me...

"Why did you leave Theos if it's as beautiful as you say?"

"Because Theosians aren't allowed to come to Earth. I don't like being told I can't do something."

We both laughed. *I just want to tell you everything.* But then I felt the smile melt away from my face. After wrenching down a gulp, I said, "I don't like to talk about it much, but my parents are...are...dead."

"Josh. I'm...I'm sorry."

"Yeah...well...space travel to Earth was their dream. They were scientists. They...they always knew it could happen. I decided to make that happen...for them, I guess."

I have her in my life. Have her...as a friend. But at least I have her. I told her some of the truth about me. How did I do that? How did I trust her? Much less anybody? But I can't talk about the age thing. Not yet. It's great having her in my life like this. But it still sucks, too, because I love her. Friendship. Guess friends will have to be good enough. I'll have to pretend it is.

A few days later, I walked into the break room, hungry. Then, right there in front of me: *Cole.*

Just what I freakin' need. I grabbed a powdered sugar doughnut from a box on the table. *Better say something. But what?*

"Hey." *Nice job, there, Josh, spitting powder on him.*

Cole cleared his throat. "So, have you heard?"

"Heard what?"

"Emma and I broke up."

Well I'll be...That's interesting. How come she didn't tell me?

"Gee, man. I'm sorry." *Am I?*

"The whole thing was a joke, a stupid joke."

"Huh?"

"You know what blows? The whole thing couldn't work...because of you."

I looked at Emma through a glass window as she sat at a computer.

"Me?"

"Yep. She never got over you. No one can compete with that, I guess."

As he left the room (no goodbye, no parting glance), the scent of fresh coffee filled the air. The coffeemaker gurgled, brewing. Suddenly, I remembered my doughnut. It tasted better. And the coffee...smelled terrific!

32

PROMISING

Holidays. Rather confusing to me. Why a day off work to celebrate something that happened so long ago? But Earthlings seem to like holidays. So Earthlings must really *like days off work...*

Columbus Day. The library was closed today, along with almost every other business on campus and in town. So I decided to ask Emma to spend the day with me. *Friends. But let's get a couple things straight: I am* not *carrying a purse or looking at nail polish colors with her...*

But plans are as easy to change as they are to make, especially when Mani's involved. I leered down at her name on the screen of my now buzzing cell phone. *Please don't let this be the usual annoying, completely unimportant, I-just-wanted-to-bother-you call.* Turns out, it was none of the above...

"What?" I hissed.

"Josh." A breathless, strained voice, graveling through. "Help me!" Her breath: labored, quick.

I barely understood her throaty whispers. "Mani, what is it?"

"I can't—" But that was all she managed before letting out a gurgle. Then the line went dead. I called her back, over and over again.

Something's wrong. Very wrong.

Within an hour, Emma and I found ourselves flying along a country road in my truck. Mid-morning. The sun shined bright through the windows. *I bet by now my truck could find its own way here to the outskirts of town—Mani and my typical rendezvous.*

I pushed out the memory of the night Mani and I hooked up. *This is about finding Mani, not a pity party with me as the guest of honor.*

I screeched around corners, faster than I'd ever driven.

"What do you think happened to her?" Emma asked, after a stretched pack tight with silence.

"I'm not sure, but it can't be good."

"What will you do when you find her?"

"Now that's a strange question, Emma. Oh...I don't know...maybe make sure she's all right?" *OK, that was rude.*

"I mean, is there something you will have to do, you know, different because you guys are aliens?"

"I'm sorry. I'll do whatever I have to do. And look: You have to promise me that you will do exactly as I say, no matter what." *If Mani was caught by humans...it's my job to protect her, no matter what. That's what a Theosian does. But I can't risk Emma either. I have to protect her, too. Can I protect them both?*

"What do you mean?"

We approached the area. I slowed then stopped along the desolate roadside. Trees all jammed together resulted in breathtaking purples, crimsons, oranges, browns; exactly why I chose Ohio: seasons. But today, they seemed eerie, not beautiful. My stomach churned.

I turned to her. "Emma, if humans took Mani, I will go after her. I'll have to."

"Well, I get that."

"You might have to forget you know me."

"What? Why? That's crazy. I—"

"Listen, you don't understand: Most humans won't believe we're harmless. They are terrified of the possibility of aliens. Don't you get it? *You don't know who I am.* Promise?

Krrrr! We both jumped. After the loud sound, we heard dried leaves rustling and wind whistling outside. Then we both sat. Silent. She sighed and looked away.

Why did I tell her anything? Now she's in danger.

"Emma, if you don't promise me, I'm taking you back to your dorm."

"OK, OK," she whispered. "I promise." Her eyes glared at me. "You happy now?"

Happy? No. "I shouldn't have called you."

"Why did you?"

She sat patiently. *She's not pushing for an answer. It's like she just understands, without words.* I trusted her...and...and...she knew it!

"We'll wait another 10 minutes, and if she doesn't show up, we'll try somewhere else."

"OK." A long pause followed. Then she spoke again: "Cole and I broke up."

Whoa. She's going there...

"He told me," I said, without looking at her. "When?"

"Just the other day, in the break room." Another big sigh. "Another one of those *mistakes* I'm so good at making."

"Don't be so hard on yourself." *Just keep me off your mistake list.*

"So, you knew, huh?"

"He just told me. I'm sorry it didn't work out." I didn't like her hurting, but did I feel sorry? No.

"Yeah." Another silent pause. "Mani and you?"

"No," I nearly shouted. "No, no, no." A deep breath helped to lower my voice, but it also made it awfully hard not to slip into an invisible form. With a little effort, though, I accomplished the former without the latter. "Consider that *my* mistake." I smiled.

"And you're looking for her now because…?"

"Because she's in trouble, no other reason." *More, Josh—now.* "It's my fault she's here. I'm responsible." I lowered my head. "She's my…friend. I have to help her."

"We'll find her, Josh." She seemed to scoot closer.

"We'll?" I like the sound of that. I glanced at my watch, realizing the 10 minutes were up. "All I ever wanted was to live on Earth. I had it all planned out. Now I've made a mess of things, and Mani's going to pay for it."

Emma looked at me. Eyes strong. So beautiful. She said to me, "I'll do anything I can to help."

33

SEARCHING

"Just wait another 10 minutes," Emma said.

"No. We need to try somewhere else. The restaurant where she…waits tables."

Why name it The Chalet? *By the looks of it, it should be* The Boring Brick Building.

Inside, plush carpeting surrounded dim tables, lit by candlelight. I squinted. A hostess wasn't difficult to find. In fact, she found us...

"Reservation? Name?"

"We're looking for a waitress who works here. Her name is Mani."

"She's off today," she said. "You might want to try her at home."

"She called me earlier today," I explained. "She sounded sick, and we were cut off. I just want to make sure she's OK. She never told me where she lived."

The hostess furrowed her brows, eyes radiating skepticism.

"It's true." Emma interjected quickly. "Mani is a friend of his, from a long time ago. We think she's in some kind of trouble. Ya know…sick…or something. Please tell us where she lives. So we can check on her."

"I'm sorry. We have a strict policy against sharing employee information."

"She might be in trouble." My voice raised a little; I realized it too late.

The hostess glared.

I don't get this. Can't this woman break a rule? It's not that hard, lady. Just as I began devising other tactics, Emma took over the conversation:

"We understand. Sorry to have bothered you." She turned to me and laced her arm around mine, gently tugging, telling me to leave with her.

As we walked away, she muttered to me, "You really need to polish your people skills, you know."

"Well, it takes two to tango," I complained in a whisper.

"Can you blame her? You can't just raise your voice and expect people to bow to your wishes."

Emma led me out onto the sidewalk in front of the restaurant.

"Emma, this is an emergency. Correct me if I'm wrong, but I thought humans understood the definition of that word."

"Well, she didn't believe it was an emergency, and just walking up to people and demanding information doesn't work."

"So now what do we do?"

"We hang out here, see what this fry cook can tell us." Emma threw a glance behind me.

"What fry cook?" I turned to look.

"The one standing outside the side door, smoking a cigarette, looking this way. I think he wants to talk to us."

I turned and looked. He was a scruffy guy, with hair hanging over his eyes, wearing an apron, smoke seeping from his barely open mouth.

"So, let's go." I started to walk toward him, but Emma stopped me.

"No, no. Just stay still. Let him come to us."

"How do you know he will?"

"He will. One more smile in his direction..." Emma completed that very task. *Voila!* One fry cook, coming right up. He ground out his cigarette with his shoe. We all met halfway.

"Hey, you say you're friends of Mani?"

"Yeah."

"You think something's wrong?"

"Yeah, we do."

OK, let her do the talking.

"Here," he said, pulling a greasy piece of scribbled on paper from his pocket. "That's where she lives."

"Thank you." Emma offered with another smile. "We really appreciate this."

He looked behind him, keeping an eye on the side door. "Well, you didn't get it from me, man."

"Get what?" Emma joked.

He ended the conversation with a wink.

Boiling, I gritted my teeth, wanting to punch the guy no matter how helpful he had been. *Get ahold of yourself, Josh. At least Emma's here with me. And she's helping me find Mani. Focus:*

Mani!

34

EMMA

"Just wait 10 more minutes," I said.

He breathed rapidly, stared at his watch. "No, we need to try somewhere else. The restaurant she where she...waits tables."

His voice trembled, but I heard more than fear in there. There was anger, too.

We pulled up to the restaurant where she worked, which was called *The Chalet*. With its red brick and gold lanterns, I felt kind of like its name didn't fit. We walked in and up to the hostess.

"Reservation? Name?"

"We're looking for a waitress who works here. Her name is Mani." Now the trembling in his voice moved elsewhere...to his hands.

"She's off today," she said. "You might want to try her at home."

"She called me earlier," Josh continued. "She sounded sick, and we were cut off. I just want to make sure she's OK. She didn't tell me where she lives."

The hostess wrinkled her brow.

She doesn't trust us. And she doesn't like Josh, like—at all. "It's true," I cut in. "Mani is a friend of his, from a long time ago. We think she might be in some kind of trouble...or sick...or something. Please tell us where she lives so we can check on her."

"I'm sorry. We have a strict policy against sharing employee information."

Before I could shut him up, Josh pushed harder for the hostess to give in. *Needs to work on his people skills...*

"She might be in real trouble." Josh's voice seemed to almost echo.

The hostess glared at us both, now. *He really has no idea he's pissing her off. Like, enough to where she could call the cops—*

"We understand," I interjected. "Sorry we bothered you." I laced my arm around Josh's, like a girlfriend would, and tugged to get him out of there. When he hesitated, I gave him wide eyes. So he gave in, let me walk him out of the restaurant. I whispered to him, "Josh, you really need to polish your people skills, you know."

"Well, she wasn't any help," he whispered back.

"Do you blame her? You can't just raise your voice and expect people to bow to your wishes." *I thought you studied Earth. What were you, a GOD on Theos??*

Thankfully, I got him out of there. We stopped on the sidewalk to take a breath.

"Emma, this is an emergency."

"She doesn't believe it's an emergency. And demanding information doesn't work."

"So, now what do we do?"

I noticed a young man, dressed in a greasy apron, standing beside a side door. He looked at and away from us several times, in between puffs on his cigarette. I smiled; the guy smiled back. "We hang out and see what this fry cook can tell us." I looked behind Josh.

Josh turned around to look at him, too.

"So, let's go," Josh said, starting to walk in the cook's direction.

"No, no. Just stay here. Let him come to us."

"And how do you know he will?"

For such a smart creature, he really doesn't get—really get—Earthlings. I tossed over another smile. *Yep, that'll do it. Here he comes.*

"Hey, you say you're friends of Mani?"

My turn to talk, Josh. "Yeah."

"You think something's wrong?"

"Yeah, we do." I said. *Don't get mad, Josh. If I don't do the talking, we might lose this guy, just like the hostess.*

"Here," he said. He reached into his pocket and pulled out a greasy paper with writing on it. Handed it to me. "That's where she lives."

"Thank you," I said with another smile. "We really appreciate this."

"You didn't get it from me, man." He looked behind him, at the door.

"Get what?" I joked.

He winked at me. Then he was gone. I noticed Josh looking a little peeved at that wink. OK, not peeved—like totally enraged. *Surely, he can let something like that go if it means we find Mani.*

35

PURSUING

Wow. What a crappy neighborhood. I can't believe she actually lives here. We passed a string of abandoned buildings, broken up by a rundown convenience store/gas station, and then her apartment complex. The brick building appeared to be pretty sturdy, and to have several vacancies; either that or the tenants preferred little to no furniture and the curtains to be left wide open. Some windows looked bare, without any curtains. I noticed a pair of cars in the parking lot, both of them old and rusted.

"Dreary place," Emma said.

I nodded. We walked up to the door and I knocked three times. No response.

"She's not home," said a voice from behind us. We turned, startled to find a young man, 19 or 20 years old, standing there. "She left a while ago. She's not back yet."

"I'm a friend of Mani's," I explained to him, stepping toward him. I noticed his t-shirt and khaki shorts. "She called me today from her cell phone. We were cut off, and I need to find her." No sense wasting time. *Hope I don't piss this guy off, too...*

"Really? You know, I've been really worried about her. She hasn't seemed...happy lately," the tenant said.

"She wouldn't tell me why, but I think she's been worried about something."

"So you guys are friends," Emma said. "Maybe you can help us."

"How?"

"Do you have a key to her apartment?" I asked.

He stood still, saying nothing, his eyebrows slightly raised.

Oh, come on. Why does it take so long to get people to cooperate? I can't stand it.

"If you do," Emma added, "we might be able to find something to tell us where she went."

Finally, his face relaxed, like a lung releasing air. "I *might* know where she went," he said, slightly hesitant.

Emma and I looked at each other, then back at him.

"At least I think I do."

Next came a pause—a silence. He looked at us. *He's studying us. Trying to decide if he will trust us. Emma's gonna need to work some charm, again. Why don't these people like me? And why don't they understand this is an emergency?*

"I'm Emma. And you are…?" she asked, stepping in front of me, toward the young man.

"Rick."

"Rick, I can see you're a really good friend to Mani."

"Yeah," he offered. "We hang out a lot."

"I'm sure you wouldn't want anything to happen to her."

"No."

"Neither do we," Emma said. "We think she might be sick."

I nodded in agreement, attempting to earn a little trust, if at all possible. His face relaxed a little more. *Emma did it again. How does she do that?*

"OK," he said. "Follow me."

We sighed in relief and followed Rick through the building's parking lot and around the back, to a field that ran along a highway, thick with trees and shrubs. He led us to a somewhat hidden path, deep within the brush, still close enough to the highway to hear the passing cars and trucks without being able to see them.

"So, you think something's happened to her?" he asked as we walked.

"I'm afraid so," I answered "She sounded…sick… on the phone. You said you've been worried about her?"

"Yeah. She's been weird lately." Rick spoke freely now. "She's been quiet, worried. Said she didn't feel right, but she wouldn't explain what she meant."

"You guys spend a lot of time together," Emma said.

"Yeah," he said. "Every day. We hang out after she gets off work. She comes out here sometimes and just sits for hours, looking up at the sky."

Emma gave me a glance. It had a question mark attached to it.

I always suspected she was homesick. She didn't seem to adjust to Earth as well as I did. Maybe I wanted to assume she'd get there on her own. Have I been…a jerk to her?

"I bet it's beautiful out here on a clear night," Emma said.

"It sure is," he said. "One time she brought her telescope and showed me constellations and stuff. She talked about the planets, like she's been to them." He said the last few words with a snicker, which evaporated after he looked down from the sky and at us. "She must read a lot of books or something."

"Yeah," Emma said. "She does. She's real smart. Is this the only place you think she might be?"

We looked around the area, without luck. *This is making me sick. I have to find her...*

"No, there's one more place over there," he said, pointing. "When they put the highway in, they cut through that hill. There are some ledges on the side of it that Mani climbs. She can climb like a mountain lion. She had to pull me up behind her." He shrugged a little, looking sheepish. He was small, for a human male, and kinda pudgy, too.

"Take us there," I demanded, and then rethought my tone. "Please, I'm really worried about her." *Watch it, Josh. Don't piss him off.*

He only answered with one word: "Sure."

As we followed Rick up the hillside, Emma glared at me. I knew what she was thinking. *Stop with the attitude or just plain shut up.* At least that's what I *imagined* she was thinking.

"There's a level spot up there," he said, pointing upward.

I had to see it, so I climbed the hill.

"Wow, he climbs as good as Mani does," Rick said.

No response from Emma.

I scaled the hillside and the ledge...then spotting her humped figure, lying on the ground. My stomach fell out of my body, it felt like. I touched her pale skin, hoping for a pulse, and then bent over her to listen for a breath and a heartbeat. *Come on, Mani. You have to be alive; you have to be!*

36

RESCUING

"She's here!" I yelled. "She unconscious. Alive, but unconscious."

"I'll call 911," shouted Rick, pulling his cell from his pocket.

"No," I yelled back.

Rick furrowed his brow.

Emma came to the rescue again: "What he means is, we can get her to the hospital quicker if we just take her ourselves."

Rick's eyes remained fixed on me as he slid his cell back into his pocket. *What's he thinking? Does he buy what she said?*

He stared at me. *Really* stared.

Why do people hate me so much today? Guess I'm not very nice when I'm upset. I climbed down, Mani packed in my arms. The three of us rushed out of the brush, to the parking lot. I eased Mani into my truck, trying to be gentle. *Anything could be wrong with her. Anything and everything.* I wanted to leave immediately, but Emma took the time to talk to Rick, something I wouldn't have thought of, much less cared to do. *People seem to like her better. Maybe I should ask her to teach me some people skills...*

"Now listen, you stay here in case any of her family should stop by, so you can tell them where she

164

went," Emma said to him. "We'll get her to the hospital right away. We'll have her call you when she's conscious, OK?"

We gave him no time to agree or disagree. I fired up the truck. Emma jumped in and off we went. Peering into the rear-view mirror, I saw Rick standing in the middle of the road, watching us drive away. His hands weren't in his pockets, but he looked so sunken and defeated, they might as well have been.

"We're not going to a hospital, are we?" Emma asked as I accelerated.

"No," I answered. "We'll take her back to my dorm room."

"Excuse me? Did you say your dorm room?"

"Yeah, that's what I said." I glanced over at her, at her wide eyes and hanging jaw. *Hmmm, I'm guessing she doesn't like my plan.* "What's wrong with that? It's a coed dorm."

"Yeah, it's a coed dorm, but how exactly do you plan to get an unconscious female past the front door without causing concern?"

Gah! I really hate it when someone else is right. "That does pose a small problem."

"Small problem? I swear, for someone so smart—"

"Don't even think of finishing that sentence," I interrupted. "Let me think a little. I'll figure it out." I drove, silent...actually refusing to talk. *Maybe we should take her somewhere else. But where?*

"Any brilliant ideas yet, Einstein?" Her grin: so adorable and yet so infuriating at the same time.

"Of course," I answered, wholly untruthfully.

"Yeah? I can't wait to hear it." She looked out the passenger side window, her words having left a cut in me.

I'll have a great plan by the time we arrive.

Only that didn't quite happen.

We parked in the dorm lot. It was a little past 11 at night. *Locked doors. Someone's on duty now. How's this gonna work?*

"Well?" Emma asked.

I had no answer.

She huffed, sighed, pulled out her phone, and began to dial.

"Who are you calling?"

"Just listen." She waited for someone to answer, then spoke lightheartedly: "Hi, is this Sherri? Oh, Misty, it's Emma. Could you check Josh's mailbox? He's waiting on an important letter."

Look at that grin. She thinks she's pretty clever. If I didn't love her, I'd be really pissed right now. OK, I don't care that she outsmarted me. I really do love her.

"No? Oh well. Thanks for looking." She hung up.

"Just what did that accomplish? I hissed.

"It told me who was on duty. I know Misty; she can't be bribed. So, we have to go to plan B."

"Plan B? You had two plans?"

OK, it's a little harder not to be pissed at two ideas. But, I'm managing.

Emma jumped out of the truck and got to work on her phone, making a number of calls.

I overheard some talk about a basement door and Misty in the front office. None of it made whole lot of sense to me. Feeling useless, I laid my hand upon Mani's cheek, feeling a slight bit of warmth. *Good sign.*

Finally, Emma put her phone away, came to my door, and told me to get out. "OK," she whispered. "You get Mani and follow me to the side door."

I opened my mouth to ask why, but found myself getting instantly shushed.

"Just do as I say or it all will be ruined."

I followed as instructed, and was soon leaning up against the cold, brick wall by the side door.

"Wait. I'll make some noise."

I soon heard an alarm bellowing from inside the dorm. Though I jumped, I remained at my assigned post. It wasn't long before Emma burst through the door from the inside and helped me pull Mani through.

We entered into the laundry room, a place I only used because everyone else did. *So stupid, how I have to "wash clothes" and "bathe" just to fit in.*

"Where's the alarm coming from?" I asked, as we struggled to pull Mani toward the stairway door.

She spoke so fast she didn't take a single breath: "The basement door's propped open; it tripped the alarm. The board in the front office lights up, showing a problem in the basement, and off they all run. It's a perfectly brilliant plan, wouldn't you say?"

"I don't know if I would say 'brilliant'—"

"Did you have a better idea?" *Ouch!* Those words, how deep they cut.

"This'll do," I answered, hoping she wasn't getting a big ego.

"God, you're such an ass sometimes," she sighed.

In the stairwell, I stopped suddenly. "How did you know that would work?"

Her lips widened, then turned up at both corners.

"You've done this before. You've snuck boys in and out," I realized aloud.

"Let's just say, my friends and I have used it on occasion in my dorm."

So, how many guys are we talking about here? I wanted to ask, but I stopped myself.

We finally climbed to the fourth floor and pulled open the door. As usual, music blared and voices could be heard throughout the hall. We both hesitated. I peeked around the corner. No one there.

I nodded at Emma; we began dragging Mani toward my room, her head flung forward, hair cascading down, covering her face. *Almost there, just one more room to get past and...*just then, who other than Stemmy stepped into the hall. *Why isn't he in Sam's room?? He's always in Sam's room!*

"Well, well, well, what have we here?" he asked as more guys came out of their rooms to see what was going on.

Oh great.

37

HIDING

"So, you're dragging a drunk one home, huh Josh?" The halls clamored with laughter. *A reasonable assumption, since most of the kids in these hallways have alcohol on their breath. How do I respond? Agree? Deny? Laugh?*

"Well, you know how crazy parties get," Emma said with a smile. "My friend is…a little sick." I eyed Stemmy, who was standing—very still—in the middle of the hall. "Get out of the way. We need to get her to my room."

The teasing doubled. I heard "Oh yeah, Josh. Two girls, all to yourself? You animal, you."

I scowled, my blood getting warm.

Emma shook her head, then said quietly: "Don't, Josh. Let them think it."

"What?"

"What's important? Mani, right? Just let it go."

So I relented, dragging Mani the rest of the way into my room. Somehow, along the rest of our walk, the idea seemed rather…interesting. A smile overtook my face, and I proudly displayed my expression back at the guys, who responded by hooting and howling all the more. *Yep, all guys are total pigs.*

Once inside, the door shut behind us. Emma shot me a look. Not a pleasant one.

"What?" I asked. "I thought you said to just let them think what they wanted?"

"Well, you don't need to...*enjoy* it so much."

I still felt my face smiling—like, *really* smiling.

We laid her on a futon. Emma watched as I felt Mani's skin, assessing her energy level. Just a little over a week ago, we'd completed the survival ritual, but her energy already appeared much lower.

I sat by her side, thinking and thinking. *How did her energy level deplete like this? Doesn't make sense.*

"There were a couple of times she managed to sneak up on me. I should have known then that something was wrong," I said, rubbing my eyes with my fingers.

Emma set a hand on my arm. "Don't blame yourself."

"Who then?" I dropped my head, still thinking. *What do I do now?*

Silence. Lots of it. We were *swimming* in it...

"Is there anything you can do for her?" she whispered.

"I can perform the ritual to try to replenish her energy level," I explained. "It should help, but I still need to figure out the cause of the symptoms or she'll just keep getting weaker again and again."

"Do you need me to leave?" she asked.

"No. You can stay...if you want."

"OK."

"It might be a good idea if you move away, just a little."

Emma backed away, taking a seat on Stemmy's bed. Although the ritual was usually performed while standing, Mani was far too weak and the floor would have to do.

A blush of pink erupted on Emma's face as I lay on top of Mani. *I'm such an idiot.* I turned to her.

"It's not the way it looks. Let me explain. You see, it's supposed to be done while standing."

"I understand," she said looking away as if suddenly moved to contemplate the posters on the wall. "Don't let me bother you. Just do what you need to."

I continued. Mani lay silent beneath me. I raised her hands above her head and held them there with mine, our faces an inch apart. I closed my eyes and— felt no sign of consciousness.

I *did* feel this swirling sense of electricity, though, gathering within me. I struggled for control as it entered my limbs, doubling in intensity.

I opened my eyes and shuddered at the sight of Mani's face, which was utterly empty and expressionless. Her body was likewise: limp and lifeless. I closed my eyes, attempting to increase the power I now forced into her body. *This…is…so…exhausting. It's so hard to do this without her awake.* But I had no choice, had to continue on. *Need to save her.* Finally, beneath me, I felt the slightest movement.

Our bodies became enclosed in an egg-shaped, golden glow. Sparks flashed like little flames, and I noticed Emma lifting her arm above her head, shielding her eyes from them.

Mani made sounds, a low set of moans not unlike a song, a haunting song. *I gotta get this over with. I don't like Emma seeing this. But if I'd made Emma leave, what would she have thought? All I know is I really don't like her watching this.*

I struggled to keep my focus on Mani. Her body now writhed, in constant motion as energy passed from me into her. Soon I sensed her energy rising. Color, returning to her face. Her face then grimaced, body contorted. *This is taking so long. Probably because she's so weak.*

I looked to my left, where Emma sat. *Where is she?* My gaze shifted over to a few feet behind me, where she stood looking on from the bathroom doorway. *She's terrified. Even a baby Theosian could read that face. But, I have to keep going...*

My back arched as we entered the final stage of the ritual. It would soon be over. The glowing dome above us brightened into a shade of yellow, then shimmered.

Mani moaned louder. A slight moan escaped from my own mouth, then we parted, both of us panting and gasping for air. I jumped to my knees, bending over her.

She opened her eyes, at first staring, as if right through me. Then, she fixed her gaze upon my face and her lips parted, curving upward into a smile.

I did it. I saved her. She's not going to die!

My neck snapped to the left, toward the sound of a slamming door: my dorm-room door. "Stay here and rest," I said. "I'll be right back."

Mani nodded, remaining on the floor, deep breaths jutting in and out of her mouth.

I scurried out into the hall, where I found Emma standing at the opposite end, her back turned toward me. *This was such a mistake. I should have known better.* I remained behind her. More teasing came from behind me. I turned around, exploding on them:

"Shut up, all of you!" Surprisingly, they did. "Just get the hell out of here, would you?" After a moment, they did that, too. I turned back to Emma.

"Emma," I whispered. "Are you all right?"

"Yeah. Why wouldn't I be?"Her voice, cracked and strained.

"I thought that might have been...upsetting?"

"It was...interesting," she said.

I'm sorry. I shouldn't have had you stay for it."

"I wanted to."

"It's quite...intense."

"Don't worry about me," she said, still hiding her face from me. "How's Mani?"

"She's all right... for now," I explained. "But, she's not cured. She'll get sick again."

"Why?"

"I don't know," I said. "We'll have to run some tests. Try to figure it out."

Emma didn't respond. For a moment, she stood still, continuing to look away.

"I'll have her stay here tonight. Tomorrow, I'll have to find another place to take her."

"Is that wise?" she asked. "She might have something contagious."

"If so, I would have already contracted that during the ritual."

"Oh."

Silence.

"Emma, what's wrong?"

"Nothing," she answered.

"Before Mani called, I was planning to talk to you about…us," I said.

Finally: Emma turned and faced me. Tear streaks sparkled from her cheeks. "You were?"

"Can we talk?" I asked. I stared into her glistening eyes, almost scared to hear the answer. I decided not to wait for one: "Now, you know who…*what*…I am."

"So?" she asked sternly. "What of it?"

"It has to make a difference to you," I said.

"What do you mean?"

"What do you think, now…that you know?"

"I don't know everything," she pointed out.

"Yeah, there's a bit more," I said. "But what do you think, now that you know the truth about me?"

"I don't see why it should make a difference in how I see you," she said.

"It *has* to make a difference," I said, cupping her by the elbow, guiding her into the stairwell for more privacy. "It's not as if you meet an alien every day."

"No, just every other day," she said. We laughed out loud.

"Funny," I scoffed.

"You act so serious. Sometimes, it scares me to think about it. But you're still the same person. I keep trying to remind myself of that." She looked out through a window, into the night. I caught a glimpse of her face, reflecting in its glass. The moonlight gleamed off her eyes, which were now refilling with tears.

"The same?" I asked. "How can you say that?"

She turned, moved closer to me. "You're my friend...no matter where you come from. You are Joshua: a kind, intelligent, and compassionate person."

"But I lied to you."

"You had your reasons," she said. "I don't blame you. Who would believe a story like that?" She caught herself. "I *do* believe you, by the way. I don't have much choice."

"I was sure you would hate me for lying."

"I do wish you would have told me sooner," she said.

"I wanted to." I leaned in toward her. "I didn't know what to do. I feel guilty about that...and about Mani."

"Why Mani?" she asked.

"I pushed her away, made her live here alone, without my help."

"Why *did* you do that?" she asked softly.

"She was hounding me," I explained. "It made me mad, but I didn't realize what a hard time she was having. I thought she was doing better than she was. But if you think about it, why should I have expected that?"

Silence again.

I stood and stepped toward the window, looking out into the night.

"I think you had every reason to want to be on your own. After all, it's not like you planned for her to come here with you. You wanted to protect yourself."

"Yeah, all about me." I sighed. "Well, it has to be different now. I'll take care of her."

She stared at me, not speaking. Her eyes spoke, though. *She's holding something back.*

"What?" I asked

"It's really none of my business…" she said.

"Just ask," I insisted.

"Will you be living as a…couple?"

"No," I answered. "I don't feel that way about her anymore."

"Josh, did you notice Rick didn't say anything about Mani being in high school?"

Quick change of subject there. "Yeah, somehow she kept both worlds apart."

At that very moment, we both jumped, startled at the sound of screams coming from my room.

"Mani!" I yelled.

I was the first to get to her. I instructed Emma to get a glass of cold water from the bathroom. I then slammed and locked the door.

After a few sips, Mani quieted down. *It could be…oh, please…please no. If it is, she can DIE.*

"It's bad, isn't it?" Emma asked, holding the water. "Is she going to die?

38

EXPERIMENTING

Over the course of a few texts to Stemmy, I managed to convince him to stay in Sam's dorm for the night. The next day, Emma called with a plan to move Mani to Kaylee's father's secluded cabin, which was located by a lake a few miles down the highway.

Within an hour we had her safely moved, and situated on a living room couch. As birds chirped happily outside in the trees, I transformed the first floor into a makeshift laboratory. A camping stove proved sufficient for providing a flame.

Emma left the room while I collected a vile of Mani's blood. Over the next couple of hours, Emma and I didn't speak at all, in fact.

Mani collapsed into a deep sleep, exhausted from the pain. I set her blood on the stove, to heat it. I then moved Mani to a bedroom and turned down the lights.

In the living room, I waited for the temperature of her blood to rise with much anticipation, knowing viscerally what humans meant when they talked about "watched pots." At one point, though, I looked away and fell into a daydream. *What if it's what I think it is? What will I do? She can't die. She can't.*

I snapped out of it when the pot started to steam. Jumping to my feet, I grabbed the pot holder. I poured some of the heated blood into a smaller container and, with an eye dropper, placed a few drops onto a glass microscope slide. I then sat, observing it at eye level.

Emma's presence occupied the space behind me. My head dropped, mouth releasing a sigh. I turned to look at Emma's face. Her eyes became glassy with tears; she sensed the news wasn't good. But she didn't say a word. The touch of her hand, firmly resting on my left shoulder, said everything.

She slid her hand off and sat on the couch, waiting for me to talk. Instead, I walked out of the room and into Mani's bedroom.

Mani had awakened, and was sitting up, sipping water from a cup. Her body trembled. She looked up at me as I entered and sat next to her.

I took the cup from her and rested it on a coaster on the bedside table.

She spoke, quietly and calmly. "What is it, Josha?"

"Its Mauck Chu," I said. I couldn't look at her.

A long pause dropped like a thud as she pondered the news. When she responded, it took me by surprise:

"It's OK," she said.

"OK?" *Was she accepting death? Maybe she didn't hear me correctly?*

"Don't be so scared," she said.

I furrowed my brow.

"I had a feeling it would be something like that."

"You knew you were sick, didn't you?"

The corners of her lips turned upward as she gazed at me. She stood up, wearily, almost falling 'til I caught her, and walked slowly to the window.

I made a leap to her side, helping her to balance.

"I guess so," she said. "It felt like something bad."

I let go of her arm and stepped back, looking at her from behind. My hands slid into my jean pockets before I summoned the courage to go to her again. I walked slowly 'til I stood only inches behind her. I could smell a fragrance coming from her hair. I looked from her to the view out the window, staring out in the same direction as she.

"I will help you, somehow," I said softly.

She turned her head. "How?" When I didn't respond immediately, she continued. "I accept it, Josha. It is what it is."

"You don't understand, I might be able to help."

She sighed and shook her head. She lifted one hand and let it rest on the window sash.

"I realize that on Theos, it means death, but here on Earth, I might be able to do something about it," I said.

"What can you do?" she asked.

"I'm not completely sure, but I think if we pair a homemade medication with our ritual, with some variations, you might be able to survive. It's worth a try," I explained.

She turned around, staring at me for what seemed more like minutes than seconds.

I might be able to figure something out. She has to let me try to help her.

"I'll think about it," she said. "Thank you."

"Mani, how did you keep your high school life and your adult life separate?"

"You figured that out, huh?"

"Yeah, not too many high school students live in apartments. How did you do it?"

"Easy. I paid someone to stand in as my parents when I needed and I didn't tell Rick or anyone else about it. I have two different ID cards."

"I see. Well, somehow we need to get you excused from school for a while by your parents. Maybe they could sign you up for digital school."

"You really think I'll be around long enough to worry about it?"

"Regardless, if not, someone will be looking for you in a couple days."

"I'll call my *parents* and get it taken care of." Then she turned back around and resumed her study of the world outside the window.

I stood there for a few seconds, thinking about all of the arguments in favor of her letting me help her. But instead of leaping right into action, I went back to the other room and sat down on the couch beside Emma.

It felt good, sitting beside her. Thoughts of what Cole had said, about her not getting over me, filled my head. *If that was true, then maybe there's a chance for us, some slight chance.*

How could I think that? Mani was in the other room, dying. *I wasn't there for her before, but now I have a chance to change all of that.*

All of a sudden, my life was beginning to be about second chances.

"Can you help her?" Emma asked.

"Maybe," I said, "if she'll let me."

"She might not let you?"

"On Theos, this disease is incurable. But Earth's atmosphere is so different. I might be able to figure out how to control it."

"I don't understand," she said. "How come you couldn't do anything about it on Theos but you might here on Earth?

"Our bodies react differently in the Earth's atmosphere," I explained. "For example, we don't have to perform the ritual on Theos, but we do here on Earth."

"How did you know to perform the ritual?" she asked.

"I studied Earth for many years on Theos. My parents were scientists. They believed we could survive on Earth, but the government wouldn't believe them."

She listened, wide-eyed. "So, the important thing is that you *can* help her," she insisted, kind of jumping the gun. "That's great."

"Maybe. If she'll let me help her," I repeated. "It's completely up to her. She might prefer to just let the disease take its course and accept death. I know it sounds ridiculous to you, but we Theosians consider the choice to die to be a sacred right."

"I want to talk to her," she said. "Choice is a right to us as well, but I'm going to talk to her."

Suddenly, she was standing. I blinked, asking, "What?"

"Leave," she said. "I want to talk to her."

"Look," I said, standing up, too, "we shouldn't try to influence her. It's completely her choice and I can't leave. I have to be close to her in case she starts to weaken again."

"I don't plan to push her to take the treatment," she said. "I just want to talk, girl to girl."

I didn't like the idea, but I didn't have to say so. My scowl did the talking for me.

"You can just wait out on the porch," she continued. "You don't need to leave the property."

"Ok," I said. "I'll be on the swing."

39

DECIDING

Inside the house, Emma sat down on the edge of Mani's bed. Their voices buzzed, soft and low. *Eavesdropping feels wrong. But how else will I hear them?*

Since I couldn't sense Mani, I knew she couldn't read my presence either. Our disconnect came from her depleted state. Meanwhile, I could barely see them through the screened window. *Invisibility? No, listening in makes me feel guilty enough.*

Emma moved to a chair facing Mani's bed. Mani looked up, a faint smile crossing her lips. Mani seemed different now, less immature and impulsive; quite serious, even, and at times mellow. Emma waited for Mani to speak first.

"Did Joshua send you in here?"

"No," said Emma. "It was my idea. I wanted him to let me talk to you."

"Let you?"

"He didn't want me to," Emma explained.

"But, he agreed, huh?"

"Look Mani, we can talk if we want to," Emma insisted. "Neither of us needs Joshua's permission." Emma rose a little, sliding back onto the edge of the bed. "If you want, I'll leave."

Mani looked at Emma, studying her face. "No...please...don't leave." Mani paused, looking out the window before continuing. "It doesn't matter if Josh gets mad at me. I had plenty of chances with him. I messed them all up." She laughed under her breath. "Nothing much really matters, once you're dying."

"No, I guess not," Emma agreed. "But hey, you're not the only one who's messed up with Josh. You and I could start a club." Emma laughed.

Mani matched the laughter. "I know how *I* messed up. What's your story?"

I winced and shuddered at the two of them talking about me. But I couldn't stop listening.

"Pretty much like yours, I think," Emma said.

"What a guy," replied Mani. "Back on Theos everyone expected he and I to...well I guess you would call it 'marry'. Maybe we were just too much alike. And then after we came to Earth, it seemed we became two completely different people."

"What do you mean?" Emma asked.

"He thrived," Mani said. "He adapted and I...I...didn't."

"He was more prepared?" Emma asked.

"Yeah," Mani admitted. "I didn't realize he was planning to escape until about a week before. It was just an impulsive decision to come on my part."

"That took guts," Emma said.

"Don't praise me," Mani replied. "It doesn't look like it was the best idea now."

"You may not believe this, but I'm glad I got a chance to meet you," said Emma.

What...is...Emma...getting...at...?
Mani breathed out, shook her head.

Emma interrupted her: "It's true. You might not agree, but I think if things could have been different, you and I could have been friends."

"You may be right," Mani said. "Josha...I mean Joshua...is one hell of a scientist, you know."

"From what he tells me, so are you," Emma said in return.

"Make that past tense. I *was* a scientist," said Mani.

"Why past tense?"

"On Theos, I was. Here on Earth, I'm not."

"You're still ridiculously smart," argued Emma. "You can still do something with it."

"Maybe...if I had...time."

"Mani, Josh told me he might be able to help you."

Mani shifted, face flashing annoyance.

"You don't have to take that help, that's up to you. But, if you do and you live, you might consider doing something with your love of science."

"You're right about it being a love," Mani said. "I do love it." A pause broke their flow. "There's no guarantee that Josh's treatment will work. It's just his best educated guess."

"Well, I've learned that his best educated guess is pretty damn good most of the time. You're smart; what's your opinion of the treatment?"

"I agree that it's the best possible course of action known. But, we are the first Theosians on Earth. It's never been done. No one knows if it will work."

"Even though science and medicine have made amazing strides here on Earth, there are a number of diseases that we just have to treat with trial and error," argued Emma.

"Yeah, I know," said Mani, looking down. "Rick told me about his mom dying of cancer. They did all they could, but she still died."

"You can certainly do what you want. I'll support you no matter what. But, it seems to me that you might as well give the treatment a try."

Mani scooted in Emma's direction. "You know, I think you're right. We might have been friends." Mani and Emma exchanged smiles...long ones. Like, *forever* long...

What the heck are they doing? They're just sitting there, staring at each other, all creepy-like.

Then, they hugged. I was sure glad I got to see that. *Very cool.*

I managed to make it back to the porch when Emma came out. She walked slowly over to where I stood, by the railing. I waited for her to begin, making sure she didn't think I was rudely fishing for information about their talk.

"That went well," she said.

"Good," I answered.

"I have no idea what she'll decide, but I'm glad we talked."

"Why is that?"

"I don't know. I guess I just felt like we should."

"Do you want to sit down?" I pointed toward the swing.

"No," she said. "I'm beat. I'm gonna go. I'll bring a few groceries when I come back tomorrow."

"That would be great," I said. "See ya then."

When she left, I sat down on the swing to relax and think. Before I knew, it I was swinging and humming an old folk song from Theos. The melody made me feel calm and unafraid, just like it had when I was a kid. I turned to investigate when I heard another voice singing along...and noticed Mani's face through the screen door.

She opened it and continued to hum with me while she made her way over to the swing.

I moved to stand, but was stopped by her raising a hand in opposition.

She sat down beside me.

"That was one of my favorite songs as a child," she said.

"I know," I answered. "I guess there isn't much we don't know about each other."

"I'm sorry I stalked you like I did," she admitted.

"It's all right," I said.

"Thanks," she said. "It means a lot that you forgive me."

"Of course I do," I said. After thinking about it, I continued, "Do you forgive me?"

"For what?"

"For abandoning you here on Earth," I said.

"It's not like I gave you a choice of whether or not to bring me," she said.

"Yeah, but..."

She interrupted: "Will you stop?"

Her volume startled me. I stared at her, wide-eyed.

"None of this is your fault," she insisted.

"I could have…"

"No you couldn't have. Look, I was wrong to stow away on the shuttle. I should have apologized long ago. It was wrong, and if I hadn't, none of this would be happening now."

I couldn't argue with her logic. *She was right, mostly. I didn't want her to come with me, never planned it, never wanted it. But, even so I couldn't just walk away without helping her.* I didn't want her, or anyone, to die. But, she had the right to decide to die. It was a harsh thought in human terms, but it was the Theosian way.

"I've decided to take the treatments," she said. The words came out effortlessly, like they were no big deal.

"Oh, all right." I tried to match her casualness. But I felt it necessary to make sure she completely understood: "There's no guarantee."

"I understand that," she said. "But, it makes sense to try."

I can't believe she's choosing this. All Theosians embrace the right of choice, especially regarding health matters, yet many of them choose to die. *Is she trying to assimilate, finally?*

"OK," I said. "We'll start tomorrow, after I get home from work."

"Don't you have class?"

"No, I'm dropping my classes," I said.

"Don't do that."

"Mani," I responded. "I think your health is more important.

"If you drop classes, I won't take the treatments. We can work around your classes, OK?"

"I'd rather be here."

"You...will go...to classes."

"All right, we'll do it your way."

She smiled. "I really appreciate you doing this for me."

"You would do it for me," I said.

"You know it." She looked at me, strong, charged with a new sense of assurance. No doubt about it, she looked like a changed person, far different from what I'd ever seen even back on Theos.

After she rose gingerly, I helped her to bed.

I slept on the couch in the living room, just outside her bedroom door. *It's up to me. She might die.*

And it's up to me to save her.

40

TREATING

I woke the next morning dreading the day head. *Emma and I both work today. That means leaving Mani. I'm gonna freakin worry all day.*

This is gonna suck.

We managed to hide our concerns over Mani well enough to do our jobs throughout the morning. But that all changed at lunchtime. So many worries started running wild through my mind, as if a cork had been pulled out of a bottle: *Is she eating? Is she resting? What if she's getting worse? How can I stay here? This is torture.*

"I hope she's all right at home by herself," Emma whispered across the small break room table.

"I sent her a text a little while ago."

"How is she?"

"She said she was fine."

"You don't sound like you believe that."

"Well, I'm sure she'll be all right 'til I get home." *You don't really believe that, Josh. Keep saying it, though; maybe you can make yourself believe it.* "You must have had some really good things to say to her last night," I said. "She seemed...different after you left."

"Different? How?" Emma asked.

"Just more…calm and maybe more…mature. I don't know, just not that stupid, immature, cocky girl she was before."

Emma shot me a thoughtful glance, lowering her eyebrows and squinting.

"What?" *She better not say that I'm immature. Cocky? Maybe. But definitely not immature.*

Finally: "I'm so glad she's letting you help her," Emma said, a little flat.

"Yeah. Me too."

Then Emma started gazing behind me.

I turned to look. Saw Cole walking toward us.

"Hey guys," he said, opening the lunch room door. "What's going on? Some big secret or something?"

"Uh…" I said gauging Emma's reaction to his question. *She's not talking. Guess I might as well tell him.* "It's Mani, she's been kinda…sick. We stayed with her…to take care of her." *What the heck? You idiot. Why did you say that? Why? Why? Why?*

Cole shot Emma a glance, studying her expression. "She's staying…with you guys… you say?" Cole quickly took a seat across from me, beside Emma, and hunched over while speaking. Great, he was now fully engaging us.

"Yeah," said Emma. "She couldn't stay alone, and she couldn't stay in Josh's dorm, so she's at a cabin. Kaylee's dad owns it. Josh and I are gonna cook for her while she recuperates."

"Josh cooks? That's a laugh. Recuperate from what?" he asked.

Emma and I stared at each other, each waiting on the other to answer. I chickened out. Or maybe wised up. After all, Emma was much better at handling people than I. "She had some kind of infection and it really knocked her out. She needs to stay with someone for a while. She gets weak sometimes."

"That's very nice of you to stay with her, Josh," he said, smirking. "Nice… and convenient."

"Cole," I insisted. "We're just friends now. I'm just helping her out."

"Can I help?" Cole asked.

"I think everything's under control," I said. *Emma's staring me down again. Maybe I said that a little too quickly. Well, whatever; he can't be coming over.*

"I'll let her know you asked about her," Emma assured him. "She'll appreciate that."

"Yeah," he said. "You do that. And I'll come visit sometime." He knocked once on the table, then stood up. Mercifully.

"She'd like that. We'll let you know when she's feeling up to it," Emma said, stiff as a robot.

"OK. Great," he said, then walked back out into the main library without saying goodbye.

"You think he bought it?" I really couldn't tell.

"I think so, for now." She gazed at him as he walked away from the break room door. "He might be suspicious, but I don't think he'll cause any problems."

"Better get back to work," I said looking down at the time on my cell phone. "The sooner the day's over, the sooner we can get back to Mani."

The clock dragged all afternoon, up 'til quitting time. Emma went back to her dorm to change clothes before meeting me at the cabin. She arrived, as promised, with brown bags full of groceries.

It didn't take us long to whip together a healthy meal of chicken, salad, and potatoes. After we ate, Emma jumped up to wash the dishes so Mani and I could get on with the treatments. This time, Emma would not to be present. Her idea. I didn't object. She dove headfirst into the detailed mechanics of dish-washing, pretending to ignore me as I underwent my preparations. I caught her glancing out of the corner of her eye as I mixed the liquid concoction and headed to Mani's bedroom. *Best to keep the noise down...for Emma's sake...*

Mani was lying on top her bed's comforter. My stomach churned as I noticed her white, pasty skin, thinned and displaying purple veins beneath. Though she lay with her eyes closed, I felt she was awake and aware of my presence. The human way. Not the Theosian way.

I breathed deeply, hoping to gain some internal control.

I set the glass of *medicine* (no other applicable term for it) on her nightstand. Waiting for her to open her eyes, I noticed the childlike quality of her features, so innocent and fragile.

"Mani," I said quietly. "It's time to start." I waited for a response.

Her eyelids finally parted, showing a sparkle underneath. She responded silently, with a smile.

"I want to start the ritual, but we will stop halfway through, have you drink some medicine, and then finish."

"All right," she answered with a very faint, weak voice. No questions. No arguments.

Wish I had as much faith in my ability to heal her as she seems to. Either that, or she just doesn't care whether or not it works.

I hope its faith.

"Can you try to stand?" I asked. "If you get weak, you can lay down."

"I can try," she answered.

"Good."

I helped her to her feet and we stood, face to face. I guided her hands to the position above our heads and grasped them, intertwining our fingers. The ritual began as usual. The energy, followed by the glow. She remained on her feet, but often closed her eyes. I liked that better than staring into them. *Why is it so hard for me to look into her eyes? What's my problem?*

The ritual went better than I predicted. She managed to stay on her feet, and we progressed well into the first 20 minutes. Her body was sturdy, and a more than ample amount of energy flowed freely between us. Her unexpected strength gave me hope, and actually bolstered my body. I felt the energy change, as expected, when we entered the next stage...

When I felt she was strong enough, I brought her arms down to her sides, pulling my fingers from their weave with hers. When she opened her eyes, she appeared to be looking straight through me.

"Mani, are you OK?"

"I think so," she said, her voice a bit stronger now. Her eyes refocused on my face.

"Sit down," I instructed.

She did, and took the glass of homemade medicine from my hand.

"What is it?" she asked, with trepidation.

"Don't ask," I said. "Just trust me and drink it."

She flung her head back and gulped the liquid as quickly as possible "Ugh," she said. "This is disgusting. Could you have made it taste any worse?"

"Can't help it," I answered. "Just sit there for a minute and rest. When I come back we'll continue."

"OK," she whispered, thumbing drops from her lips and leering down at the remainder in the glass.

I rose and left the room, shutting the door firmly, so I felt it was sealed. I turned around and entered the kitchen to find Emma sitting at the table, staring downward at a half-empty coffee cup. When I slid into the chair across from her, she didn't look up.

"How's Mani?" she asked.

"She's resting," I answered.

Still didn't look up.

I felt it necessary to fill the pause: "Thanks for doing the dishes."

"No problem," she said. She then rose and walked toward the refrigerator. "Do you want something to drink?"

"No, thanks," I answered. "I'm fine."

She returned to the table with a glass of juice for herself. "I put leftovers in the fridge, and I'll plan tomorrow's dinner."

"I really appreciate this," I answered.

Still...she hadn't looked at me.

"Is there something else on your mind?"

Finally, she raised her head...and looked right past me.

I moved my own head to catch her gaze directly.

But she looked back down at the table and sighed. "It's just..." She was interrupted by a buzzing sound. We both scurried to try to discover its origin. The buzzing continued; we ended up searching the kitchen. Emma was the first to check Mani's purse; she pulled from it a vibrating phone. We both stared as it rested in Emma's hand.

Who could be calling Mani? And more importantly: Should we answer it?

PART FOUR

41

DEFINING

"I'll answer it," I said.

"No, I better," she said, tapping on the screen. "Hello. Yes, this is Mani's phone. Who is this please?"

"Hi, Rick," she said, throwing me a stare. "It's Emma. Mani's here with us. She's still recovering or I would have had her call you." She paused to listen to him speak, and then continued. "The doctor said she had some kind of infection. I don't understand what it is exactly but she's staying here while she gets better."

"I'll tell her you called." Emma hung up with Rick and set the phone on the counter. She looked at me, scowling. "I forgot about Rick."

"I'll tell her," I said, pivoting to return to Mani.

"Josh," Emma said. I turned back in time to see her bite her lower lip. "I hope it goes well."

"Thanks."

I returned to the bedroom to find Mani sitting up. I walked toward her and waited for her to return to her feet. When she did so, we continued with the ritual. The energy returned quickly and we were finished within 15 minutes, sooner than I'd expected.

As I left her room, Mani laid down on the bed. I turned back, standing in the doorway. "Oh. I almost forgot. Rick called on you cell. We told him you were recuperating."

Mani smiled, nodded, and closed her eyes.

Emma waited in the living room, perched on the couch with her legs pulled up to her chest and her arms wrapped tightly around them. She looked up when I came from the bedroom.

I collapsed beside her. *Please let the rest of this night go smoothly. No arguing, please.* "I'm so glad that's over for tonight." I rubbed my eyes and ran my fingers through my hair. *Exhausted. Need sleep.*

"You look so tired," she said.

"I'm all right." *You're lying.*

Emma remained quiet.

Yeah. Doesn't look like she believes me. In my mind, I considered one phrase after another, unable to find the one, good opener. Before I could try one out, she spoke:

"This is all so weird," she said. "You guys used to be lovers, then you split up, and now you're in there, working to save her life."

"That's weird?" I asked, even though I knew the answer.

"Uh, yeah. Real weird. Weird, like you and me," she admitted.

"Us?" I asked. *What, exactly, does she mean by that? Maybe, I don't really want to know.*

"You don't feel weird about us?"

"No," I said. *This is about the weirdest situation ever. But I can't tell her that.*

"You don't?"

"No, I wouldn't call it weird, it's… comfortable," I said. *Careful with your words, there, Josh.*

"Comfortable?" she asked. "What I meant was that you and I were, well, kind of... together, sort of and now..." She threw up her hands and dropped them, letting them smack against her thighs.

"I don't know what we are either," I said, leaning just a bit closer to her. "But what I do know is, I can't imagine not being friends or getting to spend time with you."

We sat there silent. Her lips sparkled, calling out to me. I resisted that familiar leaning-in desire. *What are we? What does she want us to be? What do I do? Females are so complicated.*

She stared at me. "What are you thinking?"

"You really want to know?" *Clam up. Clam up.*

"Yeah," she answered. "I really want to know."

Let's see. How can I say this? "Well, I was thinking how two people can really care for each other, but not make it work because of bad timing." *Good, Josh. That sounds pretty good.*

"You and Mani?" she asked.

"No," I said, letting my eyes meet hers. "No, I meant more like you and me."

"So," she drew the word out. "You think it just wasn't the right *time* for us?"

"Maybe," I offered. "It's possible, isn't it?"

"I guess so." She stared ahead, deep in thought. "But, if two people really care about each other, shouldn't they do whatever it takes to make it work?"

"I don't think it's always that easy. Other things can get in the way."

"Like being an alien." She smiled.

"Yeah," I admitted. "Like being an alien."

"I get that," she said.

"Don't make it sound like I'm a hopeless freak." I stood up from the couch and walked to the window. *Is that what she thinks?*

"Sorry," she said gently. "That wasn't cool."

I turned back. Unable to resist that magnetic pull, I returned to my previous spot on the couch, this time angling my body in her direction. "I'm the one who needs to apologize."

"OK. Listen," she said firmly, almost interrupting me. "Enough is enough. Forget about the past. Move forward. OK?"

"I don't like you being mixed up in all of this." I glanced back at the door to Mani's bedroom.

"A little late for that, don't you think?" Emma said.

"Yeah, I guess it is. Maybe it would be better if you weren't here. You can go, if you want."

"Don't worry," she answered, while running her own fingers through her hair. "I will…if I want to, that is. I can decide that, thank you very much." She took a deep breath. "Maybe, it's OK for relationships to be muddy. You know what I mean?"

"Yeah…well…I've got plenty of mud, that's for sure. I'm surrounded in it, you could say."

"Like I do any better?" She laughed as she spoke. "Maybe it's better if we just leave it that way for now."

Her lips parted, casting pure white sensations in my direction. My heart melted as usual. I had it bad for her. *Face it, Josh. You are hopelessly and ridiculously in love with this girl. And she's right: We need to focus on Mani now. But, having both these girls back in my life at the same time...just crazy. The one I loved back on Theos lying in a bed, dying. The one I love from Earth, working beside me to try to save her. What did I do to deserve this chaos? Why me?*

42

FORSEEING

The days seemed to drag on and on, as Emma and I took care of Mani. Most of the time, Emma stayed by her side.

Mani and I performed the ritual every other day at first, then stretched it to every 3 days. To say the least, I was heartened by watching her color gradually turn from pale clay to peachy bright. She smiled more, also, but the craziest change was in her overall behavior. She started showing *appreciation* for everything we did, instead of it being all about her, like it had been in the past.

It's so hard to trust that she's really changing. Maybe it's only because she thinks she's going to die. If I save her, she might go back to her old, cocky, self-centered, self...

Emma and Mani talked alone more and more. And I of course kept eavesdropping. The conversations turned to Emma and me a lot, and I didn't like it.

Emma tidied up Mani's room for her, which always included changing her linens. Mani rested in a recliner, watching Emma work.

"You look good, Mani." Emma slid bed pillows into clean cases.

"Thanks," Mani replied. "I feel better."

"The treatments seem to be helping."

"If nothing else, they make me feel stronger." Mani paused and then continued in a different direction. "How are...you and Josh...getting along?"

After a pause: "Fine."

"Just fine?" Mani prodded.

"We're OK." Emma paused again. "He's extremely focused, you know, on your treatment."

"He's always been that way. Extremely focused, I mean. Gets his mind set on something and look out. It's good cuz he's successful. It's bad cuz it can drive a person crazy." She paused. "If you don't mind me saying, Emma, I think you guys are very good for each other."

"Oh yeah?" Emma completed her task and sat on the edge of the bed, facing Mani.

"Well," said Mani. "It's hard to explain. When you two rescued me, I realized you make a good team."

"Yeah," agreed Emma. "We were both very worried about you, Mani."

"That isn't quite what I meant," she said. Mani slid back and forth, drawing sound from the creaky, wooden rocker beneath her. "I have a feeling the two of you should...no...*must* end up together."

"Must?" Emma asked.

Geez. Now, that's weird. Mani's foreseeing the future and giving romantic advice?

Mani sounded sullen, very serious. "Some people just belong together, Emma."

Nothing. No whispers. No more movement coming from the room. *They can't just be sitting there, staring at each other.* My watch timed the silence for 2.5

minutes. *I can't stand this. This is insane. I can't listen anymore.*

43

IMPROVING

After three weeks of treatments, Mani grew even stronger. Good color. More energy. A healthy appetite. I couldn't even convince her to sit and rest. And I caught her working around the house, like, constantly.

Meanwhile, Emma started staying overnight at the cabin instead of driving back and forth, to and from her dorm. *Wonder what her roommate thinks.*

The treatments were slowing down, nearly to the point of being unnecessary. I planned to keep Mani on a short leash for quite some time though, just to be safe.

One Saturday morning, Emma slept in later than usual. I was drinking coffee, sitting on the front porch swing, when she joined me.

"Good morning," she said as she walked over to sit next to me.

"Good morning." My mind raced ahead, looking for an acceptable topic of discussion. "It's about time, you know."

She snickered. "Huh? About time for what?"

"Oh," I said, shaking my head. "Sorry. I mean it's about time we have Cole over and Mani call Rick. Especially Rick. He might just drop in, or worse. He might call the cops or something."

"That's true. I'll talk to her about calling Rick."

"I need to talk to her about not talking about certain things before we have Cole over." I blew on then sipped from my steaming cup of coffee.

"Yeah," she said. "That's probably a good idea, but I don't think you'll have any trouble from her like that anymore."

"I know. She seems different." I said. "It's like she cares…about all of us, now."

"I think it's more than that," said Emma.

"What do you mean?"

"She cares more about everything," she explained. "Before, no one else mattered. You. Me. Society. Earth certainly didn't matter to her. But, now… everything matters."

"She was a lot like that back on Theos, a very, very long time ago," I said staring out into the street. "We grew up together. She was…such a good person." I felt my throat locking up a little. Looked down into my coffee. *Don't let her see you get emotional.* "It really hurt to see her change. But then, when she changed, I got so mad at her. I just didn't care."

"You and she both are good people," Emma said. "Are all of the people of Theos like you guys?"

"What do you mean by like us?"

"Smart and kind."

"No, of course not," I said. "There are good and bad on Theos, just like on every planet. Mani started her downward spiral long before we came here."

"Every planet?" she asked.

She looked at me, a thousand questions in her eyes.

I smiled at her, realizing I'd let out more secret information.

She looked away, remained silent for a while before speaking again.

"It's OK. I know I'm not supposed to know all of that," she said.

"It's all right for you to know," I said. "It's not like you're going to blab it around. If you do, I'll be visiting you in a psychiatric hospital."

She laughed. "It just seems so weird to talk about life on other planets. So many people suspect it, but no one will talk about it. Like you said, if you do, everyone will think you're crazy."

"I don't understand that," I said. "If there's life on Earth, why isn't it possible that there is life on other planets too? But they don't want you to know."

"You mean the government," Emma said, tensing up a little. She sat up straight and planted her feet firmly on the ground, halting the rocking of the swing.

"No, not them," I explained. "Your government doesn't even know about all of the other inhabitants. You see, on some planets, cultures are good at keeping their existence a secret. They don't want anyone, especially Earth, to know."

"Especially Earth?" she asked.

"Earth is a...complicated place. So many governments and countries. Other planets stay hidden on purpose, to avoid hostility."

"I guess that makes sense," she said. "But couldn't that happen with any planet? Why Earth?"

"No," I said. "You see, other planets have shown themselves to be friendly, welcoming, to outsiders. Earth is hostile toward those they don't know or understand. Let's face it, your people can't even get along with each other."

"It's so embarrassing. But, it's true," she sighed. "I would like to think that we are accepting." Her head fell. "But that just isn't the case."

"Don't be ashamed," I said. "You can't help it. It's been instilled in you by others."

"What's been instilled?" she snapped.

"Fear," I stated. "I didn't mean anything rude."

"I know." She sighed again, rolling her eyes. "It just makes me mad that others stay away from us and we can't know about them. And even more mad to admit that some of our own people aren't accepted."

"If the people of your planet would begin to show more acceptance and tolerance for their own, then maybe those from other planets would be willing to take a chance on you, as well. But until then," I said, "it won't happen."

"Well, I'm glad you trust me."

"Me too."

I smiled. Back inside, we talked to Mani about Cole and Rick. She seemed excited about talking to her old friend. Mani sat on the couch, her cell phone to her ear. The volume must have been on high. Either that, or Rick just talked really loud...

"Rick, its Mani."

"Hi Mani," he said. "How ya doing?"

"I'm feeling a lot better," Mani said. "Josh and Emma are taking real good care of me."

"That's good. I was worried about you."

"Don't be," she said. "Josh and Emma are the best. You did the right thing helping them find me."

"You never told me about them," Rick said. "I wasn't sure what to think when they showed up."

"It's OK. How are you?"

"I'm OK. They rented out your place when you didn't come back. I made sure I got your stuff out of there. It's all boxed up."

"I'm sorry, Rick," Mani said. "I should have thought of that."

"No, it's OK. I didn't mind. So what do the doctors say you have?"

"It's some kind of an immunity problem. I can't remember the name, but it's getting better."

I was impressed. She answered his questions with ease. "I'll be staying here for some time. Need to get back on my feet."

"Can I come and see you? I could bring you your stuff."

"Yeah," she said, looking my way. "I'm sure that would be all right. But I'm not sure when. But, I'll call you back tomorrow and we'll figure something out. OK?"

"OK," said Rick.

"Don't be worried, Rick. Call me any time on my cell," she said.

"I'm so glad you're OK, Mani. I'll talk to you tomorrow."

"Bye, Rick." Mani hung up and released a pent-up sigh.

"What's wrong?" I asked.

"Nothing. I'm just realizing how lucky I am to have friends."

"Feels good, huh?"

"Yeah," she said softly.

"We can have Cole come on the same day as Rick," I suggested.

"Sounds good," she said. "When?"

"How about Thursday?"

"Thursday it is," she agreed. "I'll call Rick back tomorrow night."

44

RECONNECTING

I enjoyed the evenings at the cabin more and more. The surrounding trees rustled with a peacefulness not found in town.

I yawned and rubbed my eyes, meandering into the living room. Switching on a lamp, I noticed Emma curled up on the couch, asleep. I couldn't help but smile at the childlike pout on her lips. Her breathing, so serene and rhythmic.

After stretching a blanket across her, I entered the room where Mani slept. But, no Mani. Just an empty bed. My heart pounded as I ran from room to room, searching.

My stomach knotted into twists. *Where the hell is she? She's not strong enough to be out on her own. I have to find her!* The next few minutes felt like hours. *She's my responsibility and I let her down, again! How could she be so stupid? How could I?* Before long, my angry shouting woke Emma from her deep sleep.

My worst fears sped violently through my head. Right before I jumped in the car to search up and down every street in town, Emma yelled from the backyard:

"Josh, she's out here!"

I ran as quickly as I could through the backdoor to encounter the most bewildering sight: the two of them sitting in the yard.

"Mani," I said, panting heavily, running my fingers through my hair and down the back of my head. "You scared the hell out of me!"

"I'm sorry. I just wanted to get some air," she explained. She stared at me through a pair of eyelid slits, almost void of familiarity. "I couldn't sleep."

"Never…do that again," I said.

The two didn't say a word. They just kept staring at me, like I was some crazed idiot.

"I'm glad you're all right," I said making a conscious effort to slow the speed of my breathing. "You should come inside, out of the night air. Don't take a chance on catching a cold." And with that, I walked back into the house.

When I peered out the kitchen window, I saw the two of them talking like nothing had happened, obviously good friends. Mani's face was hard and serious.

After a moment, they stood and walked toward the backdoor.

When they came in, I said goodnight and retired to my room. With each new step, I felt an unusual heaviness in my legs, and my head spun slightly, a little dizzy. *How could I be so tired?* I struggled to get ready for bed. Each little task felt like a big job. Fighting off shakiness, I fell asleep, but I woke frequently, as in every few hours.

The next morning, I felt as tired as I had the night before. Coffee was my savior as I pushed into the workday.

With each new night, I hoped for a better night's sleep.

For several nights, I didn't sleep at all.

Thursday rolled around quickly. I managed to push through at work, despite feeling like crap most of the time. Soon the three of us prepared for Cole and Rick's big visit. Rooms were cleaned, signs of my makeshift laboratory were whisked out of sight, and Mani was sure to look her best: new clothing, new hair, new makeup; picture perfect. I sat beside her.

"Mani," I said. "You're sure you feel up to these visits?"

"I feel fine," she answered, palm on my forearm.

"As far as either of them knows, you were sick, treated by a doctor, and getting better."

"Josh," she snapped. "I can handle it." She studied my face. "What is it that you're worried about?"

"We have to protect our secret, Mani," I said. "Our safety, yours and mine, and Emma's for that matter, depends on secrecy."

"Why are you telling me this?" she asked. "You don't think I would endanger our safety in any way, do you?"

"Emma says I shouldn't worry, but..."

"She's right. You don't need to worry," she insisted. "You have done so much for me. If it weren't for you...well...you know. You came through when I needed you." She looked intensely at me. "Our secret will be forever, our secret."

I knew then and there that she was as devoted as I. I still would worry, but not about her. I'd worry about humans finding out about us. In fact, my worry, my fears in general, would seem to grow as time went on.

I shouldn't be this worried, but all I can seem to do is shake. I have to hide this. I can't let either of them see how nervous I am. I have to be strong, for them. For Mani. I feel sick to my stomach, and I'm not eating. I need to eat something. I managed to shove a sandwich down my throat before our first guest, Cole, arrived. *Just hope it stays down.*

I wondered how many hours he'd spent in front of a mirror before coming. Hair styled with gel, trendy clothes, and aftershave. Emma noticed, too; I could tell by her smile. As guys go, he was looking pretty good. Not that I cared. I just found it interesting that he would go to all the trouble. *I think he's really got it bad for her. And I don't blame him.*

His body language sent clear messages to Mani, and by my evaluation, she definitely received them. At one point, he walked across the room with her, and together they sat on the couch. After about 20 minutes of small talk, it became clear his focus was on *her*, not her illness.

Eventually, Emma nodded at me to go into the kitchen with her. That was fine by me; I wasn't exactly sure either of them had remembered we were even in the room to begin with. As the two of us sat at the table, Mani's laughter echoed throughout the house.

"Wow," Emma said with a laugh. "Would you get a load of that?"

"Yeah," I answered. "It's pretty funny huh?"

"Funny?" she asked. "It's awesome. She's having the best time she's had in a long time. Just listen to her."

"I didn't expect this," I said. "Did you?"

"No," she said. "I didn't, but it's great to see, isn't it?"

"Yeah." I couldn't help but wonder how Emma felt about Cole and Mani. "You all right?"

"Me?" She seemed perplexed. "Why wouldn't I be?"

"Any…old…feelings left?"

"For Cole?" she frowned. "Absolutely not."

"What about you?" Now she studied my face. "Huh?"

"Me? No, I'm over him!" I squawked.

She laughed. "You know I mean Mani."

"Oh, yeah," I lied. "Nope." I took a swig of pop. "If Rick weren't coming, too, I'd say we should go out for a walk and leave the two of them alone."

"Well," she said. "If Rick leaves before Cole, we could do still do that."

"Yes, we could," I answered. More laughter poured from the living room. We smiled at each other. I looked up at the ceiling and continued, "But, she's 17, Em."

"Yeah, I know. But she's an adult on Theos, right?"

"We're not on Theos. He thinks she's older. It's not right."

"I think that's her business, don't you think? It's not like they're 10 years apart. Do you know how many 17- and 18-year-olds date? Will you please stay out it?"

"I guess. I don't know. Oh…all right. I'll let her handle it," I said with a smile. Then, as a serious afterthought: "I want to be that happy."

"You will be," Emma insisted.

"How do you know?" I asked.

"Just call it women's intuition." She grinned.

"Oh yeah?" I asked.

"Yep," she said arrogantly. "We women *do* have special powers too, you know?"

"I won't argue with you there. Shoe shopping, winning every argument. Let's see, what else…?"

She hit my arm.

"Shut up."

"No," I said. "I'm just kidding. I love your optimism, though."

"You do, huh?"

We stared at each other again. Only this time, she seemed more into me than before. Unfortunately our little cat and mouse game was interrupted by the doorbell. Rick. By the time we got into the living room, Mani had already let him in and was introducing him to Cole.

"Nice to meet you," said Cole, holding out his hand. After a moment of slight hesitation, Rick reached out and shook it.

Rick really doesn't like Cole. Wonder why…

"You too," said Rick, with not much in the way of sincerity.

"Cole," she said. "Rick is a friend that I used to live beside. I want to have a few words with him, alone."

"Oh," Cole said, eyebrows crawling atop his head. "Sure."

"Come on out into the kitchen, Cole," I said.

So the three of us stepped into the kitchen while Mani spoke with Rick in the living room. Cole lingered behind briefly, and was the last to come in. When he was finally inside, Cole grabbed coffee and joined us at the table.

"Who's this Rick?" Cole asked, not one to keep his thoughts to himself.

"He and Mani used to live in the same apartment building, before she got sick," Emma explained.

"He looks a little creepy if you ask me," Cole said.

"He's just suspicious," said Emma. "I think he likes her and wonders if we're taking care of her."

"Likes her?" he said, the words riding on a slight laugh. "That's ridiculous. She'd never go for a guy like him."

"Why not?" I asked. The angry glare I got from Emma was, I admit, deserved.

"Don't listen to him, Cole. Josh is just being stupid."

"Yeah man," I said. "It's obvious she's into you...and you into her." *OK, that second part wasn't really necessary.*

Cole smiled and blushed. Not much was said after that. Mani and Rick could be heard saying goodbye, followed by the front door opening and closing. Not wasting any time, Cole rose quickly, returning to the living room. We followed.

"How did it go?" I asked Mani.

"Great. He's always been kind of protective of me. So I knew I had to talk to him alone, to reassure him."

"Did it work?" asked Cole.

"Yep," she said. "I don't think he's worried anymore."

"Good," Cole said. "Now, where were we?" He led her back to their place on the couch, which Emma and I took as a cue to vamoose.

We slipped on our shoes, exited out the back door, and began strolling down the sidewalk. We walked in silence for some time, until she finally broke it.

45

ENJOYING

"I think Cole and Mani are good together," she said. "Mani deserves a real relationship. No games."

"Is that what she said?" *What's with this 'real relationship' and 'no games' stuff? Is she talking about the same Mani I know?*

"In a roundabout way," Emma said. "Thinking about dying made her grow up."

I couldn't keep this thought from leaving my lips: "She assured me that she wouldn't ever give us away."

"I'm sure she won't."

We walked around the hillside before ending up back at the cabin. I opened the door to let Emma walk in first. We halted immediately: The sound of heavy breathing came from the living room. Emma smiled at me. We quietly backed out the same way we'd come in.

"Emma, shouldn't we be free to—"

"No. We should mind our own business." She walked to the swing. "Sit down with me."

Together, over the past couple of weeks, we'd passed quite a bit of time on this front porch. *This feels like our spot. Guess I'll think about that instead of whatever's going on inside.*

"Well," she said, winding up for sarcasm, "I guess they like each other."

"I guess so. They don't seem to be wasting any time."

"Oh," she said. "Don't get all stupid. They're not little children."

"I know," I said. "Mani will be 18 in a month. Guess I never told you that. I'm not getting all stupid." *Please don't ask how old I am. Or when I turn 18, even though it's right after Mani.*

She smiled and blushed. "None of us are little kids."

Oh, how I wish I could have a redo with Emma. Maybe I'll get one. Yeah, so I can screw it all up again?

"It's getting breezy out here," she said, clutching her upper arms with her hands.

I looked back toward the house. "I'll get your jacket," I said, starting to get up off the swing.

"No, don't." She held a hand out. "It's OK. I'll be all right."

"No," I said. "You're cold." I looked around. "I know. We can go into the garage and sit in my car."

She pursed her lips, glancing upward in thought. "Maybe we could sneak in through the back door."

"We should be able to go in if we need to," I demanded, getting a little righteous, throwing my hands up and letting them drop.

"Josh," she said, gently grabbing the front of my shirt. "I think this is the happiest Mani has been in a long time. Let her have this."

"OK," I said. 'But we're going into the garage. I won't let you freeze."

I didn't wait for an answer; I grabbed her arm and the two of us walked over to the garage and in through the service door, the breezy chill nipping at our ears.

I opened the passenger side car door for her and she entered...following a flirtatious curtsy. What had gotten into her? I joined her, sitting in the driver's seat. Soon our shivering ceased, and we took turns yawning.

"This reminds me of when I was little. I used to play in my father's garage," she said. "He never kept any tools or chemicals out in the open so I was allowed in." She smiled sweetly, eyes lit up by memories. "It was a clubhouse one day, a castle the next. It was anything I wanted it to be." She laughed a bit, her breath turning into mist.

"Sounds like you have a great imagination."

"I pretended every day," she said. "My dad called me his little dreamer."

"All amazing things, start out as dreams."

"Mmm. So, you're saying it's good to dream?"

"I think it's more than good," I said. "As far as I'm concerned, life requires it." I stopped to consider the past few years of my life. "I'm a dreamer, too."

"You?" she asked in disbelief. "The scientist? The man of facts? A dreamer??"

"If I wasn't a dreamer," I questioned, "would I be sitting here on your planet?"

"Your planet, too. But I'm saying, maybe that's more a scientific challenge?"

"Yeah, maybe. But it started out as a dream." I paused and took a deep breath, making mist of my own. "My parents were scientists. They believed our government was waiting longer than necessary to allow us to visit Earth. In a way, my coming to Earth was for them." I paused again. "So, you see, dreaming is a requirement in life, in order to get what you want out of it."

"Makes a lot of sense," she said, opening her mouth into a giant yawn.

"Stop that. You're making me tired, too," I said, matching her yawn.

After some more time passed, we tilted our seats back and relaxed. I saw her shiver a little, so I reached back to get the blanket I kept in the rear, in case of an emergency.

"Thanks." She unfolded it. "It's big enough to share." She handed me the other half, and I gladly accepted.

We reclined, our heads turned inward, facing each other. I couldn't help but smile. She smiled back. *This is happiness. This is right. Will I ever tell her that? Does she already know?* Emma's eyes drew shut. I closed my own eyes, matching her again.

I dreamed. I truly had some of my most beautiful dreams ever. Gorgeous colors swirled all around me, and turned into a countryside backdrop. There I stood, amidst the trees and bushes, a gentle breeze caressing my cheeks, dancing through my hair, filling my loose clothing like a balloon. In my dream, I also closed my eyes, and experienced this great sense of wonder.

Then, suddenly, the dream had changed. I wasn't alone anymore. Emma, in an English peasant gown, stood beside me smiling, gently and peacefully. Her clothing, like mine, flowed in the gentle breeze that eased over her skin. I'd been happy in that field by myself, but with her I was blissful, in complete contentment. I knew where I belonged. I knew it was meant to be that I would escape so dangerously to Earth, in order to fulfill my destiny. That destiny was to be with Emma.

I opened my eyes, feeling I had slept for a really long time, as measured by the pasty, cottony taste coating my mouth. I looked around and saw the sun, peeking in through the dirty, smudged garage window. Emma was still asleep. Immediately, my thoughts turned to Mani.

Just then, Emma woke. I suppose my fright and despair were written on my face, because she said:

"Calm down, Josh."

I looked at her, blinking.

"Mani's fine. She sent me a text in the middle of the night. The beep woke me, but I let you sleep since there wasn't anything to worry about."

"What did it say?" I sank into my seat, weighed down by relief.

She scowled, but it was very quick. "Um…it's kind of personal, girl talk," she said. "I *can* tell you that she is fine."

"Did Cole stay the night?"

"Josh!"

"What?" I asked. "It's a valid question. And I need to know she's physically… medically OK."

"Rest assured, Doctor, that she is both physically and medically OK. She's not experiencing any problems."

"Well," I said. "I guess that's all I need to know."

"Josh," Emma said. "You need to stop hovering over her. She needs some space. You said it yourself that she's recovering better than you had expected."

I felt my body tensing, and growing hot. "And it's up to me to see she doesn't relapse."

"You have to back off at some point," Emma implored. "Cole's a great guy. Don't ruin it for the both of them."

I sighed. *She's right. But, what if he saw her glow? Are we gonna have to tell* him *our secret too? I really don't wanna think about telling anyone else.*

It was hard enough for me to trust Emma.

46

WORRYING

After we dragged ourselves from the car and entered the cabin through the back door, Emma jerked my arm. "Remember, Josh," she said. "Act normal. She's not a kid!"

"Message received, loud and clear," I responded, forcing a smile.

We found Mani sitting on the couch in the living room, alone. She looked showered, wore fresh clothes. She looked at us meekly as we entered.

"I feel so gross," Emma said. "I can't wait to shower."

"Thanks, you guys," Mani said. "I appreciate you both giving me privacy last night."

"Of course," said Emma, speaking for the both of us. "We were glad to see you laughing and having a good time. And besides, now you owe us big time." Emma laughed and went off to shower in the guest bathroom at the end of the hall.

I retreated to another bathroom, which was situated off the bedroom I used. After I showered, I found the two of them in the kitchen, preparing lunch. They ate and talked normally. I didn't talk much. I was too busy thinking. But I was also observing. Observing how healthy Mani looked and also, how…happy.

Afterward, Mani and I disappeared to her bedroom for a treatment. She sat on the edge of the bed, sipping her medicine. I stood, leaning against a dresser in front of her, looking down with my arms folded in front of me.

"So," I said. "I guess we should talk about Cole."

"Why?" she asked.

"Well," I said, smirking. "It appears the two of you are getting close, and I thought we might need to discuss what to do about our secret."

"Josh," she said adamantly. "I promised you I wouldn't tell and I didn't."

I looked out the top of my eye lids, not offering any words for a moment. But, she knew what I was thinking.

"Yes," she said, a blush spreading across her cheeks. "I know how to hide the glow. You're not the only one who can."

"*Me?*" I joked. "I don't know what you're talking about." We laughed together. "Seriously, I really meant that we might have to consider letting him in on things."

"I thought you said—"

"I know what I said," I interjected. "But that was before I realized how serious you two were becoming."

"I think we better hold off on that," she said. "Let's just wait and see if this goes someplace, OK?"

"Whatever you say, but I think you're going to end up being faced with it."

I took the empty glass from her. She stood up to face me, getting into position. Her look was serious; happy, but serious.

"How do you know?" she asked.

"Let's just say...it just has the look."

"What do you mean?"

"You know exactly what I mean," I said with a smile. I raised my hands above my head; she did likewise. As I looked into her eyes, I could tell that she knew exactly what I meant.

We began the treatment process. I waited for her to close her eyes, then did the same.

Halfway through, I began to feel weak and slightly dizzy again. *Give me a break. Won't this damn bug ever go away? Try to ignore it and finish, Josh.*

Nearly at the end, I opened my eyes to find Mani staring directly at me. Her mouth hung open; her brows furrowed.

"What's wrong?" I asked.

"Nothing," she said. "I was just thinking about what you were saying. You know, about Cole. That's all."

We lowered our arms. "You feel all right?" I asked.

"Yeah," she said. "I feel great; strong, in fact."

"Good. Well...I don't think we'll have to do this for at least a week."

"Cool."

She and I left the bedroom to rejoin Emma, who was putting away the last of the dishes.

"How's it going?" asked Emma.

"Excellent," I said. "She won't need another treatment for at least a week. I can tell she's getting stronger from her vibe."

"Her vibe?" asked Emma.

"He means that the signal I'm emitting, the one we use to sense each other's presence, is strong."

"Right," I said. "That's the easiest way to know she's recovering. Before I knew she was sick, she snuck up on me a few times."

Mani laughed at the memory.

"That can't happen anymore."

"So you sense me strongly?" she asked.

"Yep," I said, "strong as ever."

Emma was smiling, but as I looked away from her, I caught sight of something unexpected: Mani dropped her head, and that concerned look she'd had in the bedroom came back. For the rest of the day, Mani remained unusually quiet. She sat reading for most of the afternoon and evening. Later on, without a word, she rose and returned to her bedroom.

47

EMMA

Josh and I kept warm in the garage, in the car, with both car seats reclined. My head rolled to face him. He faced me, too. *Mani is very, very happy right now. I'm glad for her. Is Josh? Or is he having trouble dealing?*

Not wanting to talk anymore, I closed my eyes to get some sleep. A few minutes later, I opened them to find Josh sleeping. I stared at his face. *I love him so much. I think he loves me. He acts like it, most of the time. Alien. He's an alien, Emma. Why doesn't that scare the crap out of you? It should. I need to sleep.* I slept.

I woke. *Still looks dark through the garage window. Why am I awake?* I felt a vibration in my pocket, heard a faint beep. *My cell. Mani.*

Where are you guys?

Josh and I r sleeping in the car in the garage. We're fine. R you ok?

Yeah. I'm fine. Well...more than fine. Lol. Sry 2 run u out.

No prob. Happy?

Very.

Get back to Cole.

Ok. Thks.

C u in the morn.

Josh didn't wake. He never moved. *Maybe we can try us again. Why can't I get used to the alien thing? Maybe I just can't get hurt again. Oh, I don't know what to do. I only know that I love him.*

We rejoined Mani in the morning. She looked fresh, showered. *I'm not going to ask her anything. I need a shower. I'm not even going to ask her about Cole during lunch. If she wants to talk, she will. I hope Josh can leave her alone.*

The treatment went quickly. "How's it going?"

"Great," Josh answered. "She's not going to need another treatment for at least a week. I can tell she's stronger from her vibe."

"Her vibe?"

"He means that he can sense I'm stronger."

"It's the easiest way to tell. Before she got sick, Mani snuck up on me a few times. That's not happening, anymore."

Mani rose and began to walk toward her bedroom.

48

DREAMING

"I'm beat." Mani yawned. "I'm gonna turn in early."

"Ok," said Emma. "See you in the morning."

Emma waited 'til Mani was in her room with the door shut before talking to me:

"Did you talk to her about Cole knowing?" she asked.

"Yeah," I said, not looking up from the book in my lap. "She said we should wait and see if it goes somewhere first."

"That might be smart," Emma agreed.

"Don't you think it *has* already gone somewhere?" I now looked up.

"Josh," she said, turning to me. "She wants to wait and see if it's going to last. I don't blame her. Telling the secret is a huge step. It's a part of her she doesn't want to give to just anybody. And I still think you should let her figure things out on her own."

I understood what she meant, completely. *But, somehow I just know they are going to stay together. They seem really connected...like Emma and me. But, it's not like Emma and I are the perfect couple. Heck, we're not a couple, at all.* But, I knew I could trust her. *I really trust Emma. Trust...and...love...*

"Josh, you look pale. Are you sure you're feeling all right?"

"Yeah," I answered. "It's probably just the horrible night's sleep in the car."

"Yeah," she said, hooking her left hand around her left shoulder to rub it. "Tell me about it. I've got an awful pain in my shoulder."

"On the other hand, I wasn't feeling too good yesterday, either."

"I thought you've looked a little under the weather," she said.

"I think it's all the worry about Mani."

"Like I said…" She got up to wipe off the counter and switch on the nightlight above the stove. "She's getting better, so you need to quit worrying so much about her and start taking better care of yourself. Eat and sleep, and most importantly, *quit worrying*."

"You're right." I smiled. "You are so right."

That night, my dreams were completely different from the previous night. The colors were bold and fire-like. My stomach churned as I dreamt of chaos and turmoil. I never really saw a discernible figure. I just knew from the sounds and the colors that it was violent, sickening. *Where're the happy dreams? The fields? Emma? Happy? What happened to that?*

I woke at least 3 times that night, each time feeling like I was about to throw up, and half-wishing I could so that maybe I would feel better. Each time I fell back to sleep, the dreams were the same. Fire, red, orange, black. Then just blackness, all around me, surrounding and engulfing me 'til there was no hope of finding my way back to a peaceful place, wherever that was. Gosh, I hoped there was a peaceful place somewhere.

I heard vague voices. Tried to recognize them, but in my fire engulfed state, I couldn't tell who they belonged to. I felt alone, lost. My head throbbed, and the churning in my stomach made way for sharp, knife-like pains. My eyelids felt heavy, so heavy I couldn't budge them. I had no choice but to surrender. I was helpless. So I gave up, let my legs and arms relax, and allowed my body to go limp.

49

SUFFERING

The next thing I remembered, Emma and Mani were bending over me. I felt like I was gonna ralph, like my stomach was churning in circles. Moreover, I was short of breath, and looking through a blurred set of eyes. *I guess I'm alive. But, what's going on with me? Maybe I won't be alive for long....*

There I lay, before the two of them, watching their mouths move but not hearing the words, which were too muffled and muddled to decipher. I looked from one to the other, hoping their words would magically magnify. Finally, Mani held up a paper with writing on it. She was asking me, in writing, if I could hear them. I shook my head no.

Again, with the paper, another question: asking me what they should do. I didn't know what to tell them. Mani wrote again. Said she had an idea. I just nodded in agreement. *What else can I do? I guess I'll know pretty soon if I'm dying or not.*

Mani left and came back with a glass that contained a liquid substance. After a couple of attempts to find the glass with my hands, fighting against the blur, I drank it down. Either it was tasteless, or that sense was on the brink too. Then I waited. Nothing happened. I drank some more. Again, I waited. Emma caressed my arm as I did so. *Glad I can feel that.*

My stomach felt calmer. Their faces, less blurred, but I felt very, very tired. My eyes closed, and I struggled to open them. Mani wrote for me to sleep. I closed my eyes one last time. Didn't dream. Just slept.

When I awoke in my bed, I could hear the traffic outside my window clearly. In the living room, the television was on. *I can hear that too.* I sat up. *I can see.* I can see!

I gingerly stood up. No dizziness. I walked a couple of steps, one foot in front of the other. *Stable.* I opened the door and walked into the living room, where Emma and Mani sat. Mani noticed me first and jumped up; Emma followed right behind her.

"Josh," said Emma. "You're awake. Do you need something? Are you all right? How do you feel?"

Too many questions, so I just picked one: "I feel good."

"Come," said Mani. "Come and sit down."

"I want to stand."

"All right," said Emma.

I stood still for a few minutes, and managed a smile, when I realized for certain that I was all right. "There," I said. "You see? I'm fine."

"Josh," said Mani. "Come sit down. I want to talk to you about something."

This time I obeyed. I sat in between them. They peered at me with cat-like expressions, serious and severe. *Now what?*

"I'm fine," I repeated, wanting no further input.

"Josh," said Mani. "I've been noticing some things, about you. You've been weak and dizzy, huh?"

"Yeah," I said, "but it's just…"

"And sick to your stomach?"

"OK," I said. "So what?"

"You look pale," said Mani.

"So?"

"Josh…" Mani said. "I had those same symptoms before I collapsed."

I squinted at her. *What is she saying?*

"I think you're sick because of me. I mean, you got it from treating me."

"But…" I started.

"Is that really possible?" asked Emma.

Mani jumped in before I could speak: "Don't argue. And don't lie to her. You know I'm right. It's more than possible. It's probable."

Crap. She's right. I could have weakened from doing the treatments. There's no way of knowing for sure, though. It's not like I have past case information. But if that's the case, how will I be treated? Mani's just barely out of the woods, and we're the only two Theosians on this planet. We can't both survive this.

"Maybe," Mani thought aloud. "Maybe you won't get worse if we stop treatments."

"That's ridiculous," I retaliated. "If you need treatments, I will give them."

"Both of you, stop," Emma cut in. "The only thing we can do is wait. Mani, you might not need any further treatment. And Josh, you might not become ill again. So…we wait."

Mani and I nodded in agreement. *Mani and I have IQs higher than any human ever, and* Emma's *the one making the most sense right now.*

The days went on. Emma and I went to work and classes. Mani stayed home. Everyone seemed fine. The longer this went on, the more relieved we all became. Soon, two weeks passed. Mani looked healthy and strong. Rick called her several times, and she finally told him she would not be coming back to her old apartment building. Emma went back to sleeping in her dorm, but spent most evenings with Mani and I at the cabin. *What would we do without this cabin? Kaylee never asked anything. She just trusted. Friends. Mani looks strong. I feel better. Thanks to friends.*

The sun, warm and soothing on my skin, covered me like a weightless blanket while I swept leaves from the porch. The air was fresh, my mind at ease. Mani and Emma laughed inside; I heard them through the porch window. The day was perfect and calm; no worries. Just as I noted the day's perfection, I heard a car pull up. I looked up and saw Cole parking and hurrying out the door.

I smiled and waved, but saw no smile from him in return, much less a wave. "Hey, Cole." Yep, he ignored my greeting completely.

"We need to talk," he barked. Then he stood there, staring at me.

"In the garage," I said, and so we walked in that direction, silent. *What now?*

I walked in through the service door. He followed. I leaned up against a workbench but he paced, looking down and wiping his brow.

Come on, dude, you're making me nervous.

Finally, he started talking.

50

LYING

"I really don't understand something," he said.

"What's that?" I asked.

He hit me with a single word: "Mani." Then: "She's better now, right?"

"Yeah," I answered. *Is he just worried about her health?* "She's all right. Really, you don't have to be all worried anymore."

"That's exactly why I *am* worried," he explained.

What the heck is he saying? "You're worried because she's better?" I asked facetiously.

"Yeah," he snapped. "If she's better, why does she insist on living here with you guys? I mean, what's up with that?"

"Oh," I said. *Oh.* "Well, maybe she wants to be extra sure she'll be OK," I lied. "Cole, it was serious. She had to quit her job. Kaylee said she's welcome to stay as long as she needs."

He stared at me. And he stared. Then, um...he stared some more.

Does he know I'm lying? He looks like he knows. Do - not - admit - you're - lying. "That would make sense, except I asked her to move in with me. Why wouldn't she do that if she couldn't afford her own place? Why here?"

My eyebrows drew close together, nearly touching. "What did she say when you asked her?"

He looked away, pacing back and forth. Wiped sweat from his brow with his hand.

I think he's all wound up. Play it cool, Josh.

"She said she'd have to think about it. And she really liked living here." He stared at me again. "Emma's not staying here anymore, is she?"

Come on. Come on, Josh. Think of something. "Look, Mani's not the type to just move in with a guy because she can't afford to live on her own. She has her pride, man. And Emma still stays quite a bit, anyway."

"But," he said. "She doesn't stay every night."

I stood up straight and walked toward him. "I've talked to her about it." *How am I lying like this? I'm getting better!* "I didn't want her to think she would be thrown out, but I thought it wouldn't look right, so I did bring it up to her."

"What did she say to you?" he asked.

I looked at the ground. "I didn't push her to make any quick decision." I regained eye contact. "I just told her to think about it, that's all. Don't push her into moving in with you. Don't you want her to because she wants and feels ready, instead because she has to?"

He thought. He nodded. *OK, he's buying it. Now I need to make sure Mani knows about the talk I lied to him about.* "Let me talk to her again. I think I can make some headway and then you come in, OK?"

"What if she heard me pull up?" he asked.

"I doubt she did, or she would be out here by now, wanting to see what's going on," I answered.

"That's true," he said.

"OK?"

He did some more thinking, then nodded again. I patted him on the shoulder as I left the garage, then ran full speed toward the house.

I threw the back door against the inside wall as I hurried in, wanting to get straight to Mani. I soon found her and Emma on the couch in the living room, looking at fashion catalogs, faces lit up with smiles and laughter.

"Hey," I said. "Listen. Cole's in the garage." I planted myself on the coffee table, facing them.

"In the garage?" Mani interrupted.

"Yes, in the garage," I said again. "He's upset because you're still living here. He doesn't understand why you're living here if you're better."

The two of them sighed at the same time, in such strong sync that it seemed rehearsed.

"I told him I talked to you about it because he was thinking something, y'know, was up, between you and me."

"You and me?"

"Yeah, and he's coming in soon," I said. "You have to let on like I've talked to you and that I want you to make a decision."

"OK," she said, after a moment of processing.

But I still didn't think she completely grasped the seriousness of the situation. In any case, we really didn't have the time to discuss it further.

Just then, Cole walked in through the front door.

"Anyone home?" he called out.

"In here," Mani yelled. He walked into the living room to join us, smiling at Mani. He then leaned over and kissed her gently on the cheek.

"Hi Cole," said Emma.

"Hi Emma."

"Well," I said. "You two have plans today?"

"I thought I'd take Mani out for dinner."

"Oh. Cool," she said. "Just let me change." Mani jumped up and skipped off to her bedroom like a schoolgirl.

"Well?" he asked after she shut the door. "What did she say?"

"She just listened again," I said.

Cole sighed.

"I told her she had to make a decision."

"Thanks man," he said.

"Hey. Be patient. She had a pretty scary thing happen to her. I think she's just feeling a little…uneasy about it."

"I guess," he said.

Emma got up, smiled, patted him on the shoulder like I had in the garage, and walked out. I followed her once again to *our place* on the porch.

As the two of them left for dinner, we were still sitting on the swing. Mani walked out, wearing one of Emma's dresses. *I remember Emma wearing that. She looked great in it.* The two of them liked swapping clothes. It seemed to be a human female thing.

"You know," said Emma. "She *does* need to move out."

I spun my head toward her.

Well, that's the last thing I thought she would say. Is she jealous? She must have read my mind...

"I mean," she continued. "It does look weird, and maybe it's best the two of them have some privacy, if you know what I mean?" She gave me a smile.

"Yeah," I stammered. "But, what if she gets sick again? And don't you think Mani should live where she feels the most comfortable? Maybe she doesn't feel right moving in with Cole?" *Plus she's 17, too. gosh, this age thing is driving me crazy.*

"We'll have a system of checking in every day. Maybe several times a day."

Has she thought this thing through? She actually has a plan?

"She needs to be independent again. It's best for her, right?"

"Oh, right," I said, but didn't really mean it. *So, she's thinking about what's best for Mani, huh? Well, I can play that game too.* "You're absolutely right. I kind of miss dorm life. I've been thinking that things have been crowded around here the last couple of weeks."

Emma looked down and then away. "Didn't mean to crowd you," she said under her breath.

"Emma," I said, immediately regretting my childish game-playing. "I didn't mean it that way. But you did say that I needed to take care of myself for a change."

245

"You do," she said, not looking up yet.

How do we handle Cole? Do we tell him everything, or do we just hope Mani can hide all her oddities?

"I wonder how she wants to handle Cole," I said. "We may have to tell him."

Now she looked at me, jaw gaping. "She's not going to want to tell him, not after the speech you made about keeping the secret."

"But, if she moves in with him," I said, "I don't think she'll be able to hide *everything* for very long."

Emma didn't answer. We just sat, in silence. *This doesn't feel...awkward. It's nice and peaceful. I love just sitting with Emma. Being with her.*

As night fell, Emma went back to her place and I fell asleep on the couch while watching reruns of old movies on TV. *Wish we had reruns back home. Oh, yeah. This is my home, now...*

Then I was out.

As I woke, I couldn't help but cup my head in my hands, trying to control a sudden onslaught of anguish. My back hurt, and I soon realized why. I sat up and found myself on a concrete floor instead of the couch. I had a pair of slits where my eyes belonged. Through them, I took note of the damp walls and darkness of my present location. *Where the heck am I? I fell asleep on the couch. Did I sleepwalk? What is this place?*

I staggered to my feet, braced myself against the rough wall, and then slid my hand against it, as I attempted to walk toward a vague light. *This isn't a dream. Where am I?*

Soon I saw a window, small and obscured by a film of mud. A tiny amount of light came in through it, but I couldn't make out anything outside of it. *I feel like I've been here a long time. I'm sweating and my breath...gah...it tastes like crap.*

I slid my hand into my pocket, but came up empty. No wallet. No cell phone. Whoever brought me here didn't want me to get away. My stomach ached; throat burned with thirst.

Giving up on the window for now, I staggered toward the cellar's opposite end to find a tiny container sitting out in the open. *Looks like I'm supposed to find this.* The liquid inside looked like water. I smelled it, dipped my finger into it, and put my finger in my mouth. Fresh. Cold. The burning in my throat was worse; it felt like tiny knives every time I swallowed. *I'm too thirsty. Have to take a chance.*

I gulped it down without another thought. Wiped my mouth, deciding to save some for later. I looked left and right, and all around the room. *Who would do this to me?*

Where am I???

51

SURVIVNG

I felt the cold dampness of the cellar floor seeping into my skin. The wooden box I used for a chair kept the chill as far away as possible. *When the sun goes down, it will get colder.* I searched the area for...well...anything I could use either to survive or escape. *And maybe I can find something in this hole to figure out where I am or who brought me here...*

The first corner...empty. But I found boxes of musty linens in the next. Along with a rusty toilet, rough but functional. *Should I be grateful for that?* In the third corner sat boxes of old pots and pans, and in the last, a metal pitcher of water.

Huh! To think I once thought I'd never need those survival training lessons back on Theos. Think, Josh. You can remember them. I took up a pot in my hand and, using the handle, marked the wall with one strike. "Lesson #5: Physically mark each passing day." *Useful in fending off the crazies, according to my old professors.*

My captor hadn't left me much in the way of clues. *At least they didn't try to kill me. No sign of wounds on my body. Once knocked out, I was at their mercy.* Meanwhile, both the toilet and the water pitcher were clues my captor wanted to keep me alive and somewhat comfortable, even if imprisoned.

I noticed the light from that dirt-filmed porthole of a window growing dimmer. Nighttime was closing in. As I yawned, I remembered another survival tactic: Thinking of something that calms one or brings one happiness. *Sure seemed stupid in our classes, but now I know...it helps.*

One corner of the basement was slightly warmer than the rest. Wasn't sure why that was, but I decided to take advantage of it. I found myself squirming around on the concrete, trying to conform to its flatness. My head, cushioned (if you could call it that) by a rolled-up tablecloth from a stale box of linens, throbbed slightly. Another tablecloth served as a sheet. I took deep breaths as I tried to relax.

I thought about my friends. *Yep, I really miss them.* My parents. *Really miss them, too.* And Emma. *Ah. Yes. That's the one. I'll be thinking of her a lot 'til I get out of this mess. She'll keep me sane.*

Her hair. Her scent. Her soft skin. Her smile. They all calmed me, somehow even bringing a smile to my cold, trembling lips. Soon those very thoughts put me to sleep.

When I opened my eyes again, I squinted at a ray of light emanating from my one and only little connection to the outside world. At least I could kind of see out the window. I sat up and eventually got onto my feet. Surprisingly, my back wasn't too sore from sleeping on the hard, damp floor. *But I hope I don't need to sleep here for many more nights...*

Stretching and walking toward the toilet, I wondered if my kidnapper was in the structure above me, or had abandoned me altogether. After I relieved myself, my eyes gazed upon a curious sight. In the corner across from me was another pitcher, a tray...and something else. I stepped closer to see that on the tray was a sparse breakfast plus two additional items: a notebook and pen.

I don't see the point of this, but I am hungry. I wasted no time eating, as my stomach ached with a deep hollowness. The water again tasted fresh and cold. I stared at the notebook and pen. *Does he really think I would want to journal? Or could I use this in some way to contact the outside world?*

Giving up on the notebook, I made sure to mark a second day line on my concrete tally sheet. I then found my wooden box again, this time cushioning it with one of the linens before sitting upon it.

Can I find any way to get out of here? Stay calm, logical, and practical. When I found doing so hard, I quickly changed from thinking about escape plans to thinking about Emma. *She has to be worried about me. All of them. Oh yeah, Cole. I forgot about the dilemma with Cole. Would Mani tell him our secret or not? I really need to know. I suppose I'll find out for myself, when I get free!*

52

REMEMBERING

The second day dragged on, worse than the first. My mind flip-flopped between thoughts of how to escape and comforting thoughts of Emma. *I'm an alien. They are just humans. Why can't I figure out how to escape from this dump?* But no matter where I pushed or pulled—with all my strength, no less—nothing budged. Nothing. *How did he do this? How did he capture me and find a way to keep me captive?* When I became too frustrated, I once again turned to Emma to sooth the pain in my head.

The eeriness of the cellar seemed to wear off a little, as I settled in for another night. I found it easier to drift away this time, still hoping for a better tomorrow.

That night, I dreamed of Emma. Sitting on the porch beside her in the swing, day after day. My body, trembling when she's near. The curve of her face. The softness of her lips as we kissed. *Why think of anyone or anything else? Well, escaping to get back to her might also be good to think about.*

Shaking. My body went from trembling to shaking, then to twitching. I woke. My eyes snapped open. *That's right. I'm in this disgusting cellar. Rather be back in my dream, for sure.* I raised my head, looking toward the wooden beams on the ceiling. *Footsteps! There's someone upstairs!*

I jumped to my feet. Shaking the cold from my body, I ran to the corner containing the wooden boxes, swooping up one of them with both hands. I held it high above my head. Then, with all my strength, I slammed it down to the floor, shattering it into several pieces. I chose the sharpest edge and held onto it tightly, while stretching it out in front of me as a weapon.

Which direction do I face? Nothing even remotely looks like a door in this place. Just how were they getting the food and water in here? And more than that, how could they do it without waking me?

I jumped and gasped: a different sound. *An engine? Yeah, it's an engine.* I listened to the sound of a car engine coming from outside the window; the car started and went either forward or in reverse. I listened as it drove farther and farther away, eventually disappearing completely. My breathing slowed. Shaking subsided. I laid back down, clutching my weapon underneath my sheer covering.

The next morning, I arose with impatience. *This is getting old,* I thought as I marked the third line on my time tally. I took a deep breath, a horribly fowl one, and looked over to see if I, once again, had food. *Yep.* So I ate my fill, and stopped abruptly at the sight of the notebook, lying open now...and containing a written message. My heartbeat quickened as I leaned over to read the scroll. A question, written boldly onto one of its pages, stared back at me.

I read aloud in a whisper: "Why did you have to take her away from me?"

My mind raced, trying to process this new bit of information. My thoughts, of course, went right to Emma. But I knew of no one who would think I took her away, and more importantly, I hadn't taken her at all. *I never actually had her, did I? Who would feel this way? It couldn't be Cole. Not my friend, Cole. Besides, he was with Mani the night I was taken away. It can't be him.*

Are you sure the note is talking about Emma? I turned my thoughts to Mani. Shut my eyes, trying to push away the very real possibility that my kidnapper may have taken Emma or Mani. I rubbed my eyes, pushing back tears. *Stay focused, Josh. It's a possibility, not a reality. Even so, my new pen pal seemed upset over not having the female in question, so chances were pretty good that I was the only one being held captive.*

Held for three days now. *Someone's sure to miss me. Someone, at home or from class. Someone must be looking for me.* But my only chance at doing something for myself hinged on the use of this notebook. *Why does this person insist on communicating with me? To make me think one of the girls might be in danger? How…how do I use it to my advantage?*

I walked across the floor. Slowly and begrudgingly, I picked up the notebook and pen. After a moment of hesitation, I flung myself down over a crate and began to scrawl onto the page. Anger and disgust poured from my fingers and onto the paper: "I have no idea what you're talking about," I wrote. "I didn't take any girl away from anyone." I wasn't about to miss my chance, so I continued: "Kidnapping is serious. Let me free so we can work out this misunderstanding."

I'd rather tell him he's really pissing me off, and that the first chance I get, I intend to rip his face off with my bare hands. Meanwhile, it sickened me to think of waiting 'til nighttime before my message would be read. *But maybe not,* I thought. *Maybe, if I make him think I'm sleeping, he might make a move.*

I waited for what I guessed to be about two hours, rubbed my eyes, and made myself comfortable in my makeshift bed. Not planning to actually fall asleep, just to make it look that way.

Then: Nothing. Not a noise. Nothing happened. I allowed my body to rest a bit before getting up, only to find the notebook and pen lying in the exact spot where I'd left them.

53

FIGHTING

I kicked a crate across the floor, satisfied by the crashing sound as it hit the wall. *I have to wait 'til tonight to try that again. I don't know how much longer I can stand this, being locked in. The walls feel closer every minute. I could smash open that tiny window, but I can't fit through it. Besides, I must discover who's doing this to me!*

As I raised my eyes toward the ceiling lined with wires and pipes, I felt a thunderous rush deep in my chest. It shot up my throat and out my mouth. *It's not like screaming helps anything, but it sure feels good, letting out three days of frustration.*

I laced my fingers together behind my head and stretched, experiencing something completely unexpected—relief. *How crazy! I'm not free, but I feel a kind of freedom.* Not physical freedom, but mental freedom. My breathing flowed easier, lighter. *I'll just sit here on my crate and enjoy this feeling.*

That didn't last long. I need to do something else. I can't keep screaming, or can I? I searched the room again for a door or opening, or anything that might even look like one. *None. This will drive me insane, if I don't get busy doing something. I know. Exercise. I'll exercise.* Jumping jacks, push-ups, and running in place, all helpful. Fatigue felt better. *I'm sure to sleep better tonight.*

I did.

It seemed like in no time at all I found myself eating my morning meal from my tray, reading my pen pal's response in the light from my dingy window. *Wow. He wrote a lot. And he didn't hold back, either.* I read the lines several times to gather as much information as possible. *Whoever this girl is he thinks I stole from him, he had it bad for her. He still loves her. It has to be Rick. And the girl...Mani. It just has to be. So, he thinks he had her, and I'm the reason they parted? Rick sure is twisted if he thought their friendship was more than just that.*

I stopped to think. *Maybe they were more than friends. They both kept a lot of secrets. Huh. I wonder...*

According to the writer, I was to blame for bad things happening to this unknown female, plus anything that happened in the future. *Crazy. He blames me for her getting sick. Well, it kind of is my fault...my fault I didn't catch it before she got bad.* According to him, my selfishness was the root of all of her problems. *Since I'm to blame and I deserve to be locked away, I don't think the chances of him considering my offer are good.*

I read the last sentence the most times, over and over. *How can a few words make me so sick to my stomach, and scared—unbelievably scared?* The writer made one thing very, very clear...

I know all about you. I know all there is to know about you and your secrets.

PART FIVE

54

EMMA

Mani, Cole, and I sat quietly on the cabin's living room couch. Everything around the room, left exactly as the day before. *Why do I keep looking at the doors? It's not like he's going to just magically walk in as usual. I can't believe he's gone, vanished. This can't be.* We sat, all of us, looking down at the floor as if it would somehow tell us how to find him. *Two days. It's been two days!*

He didn't choose to leave. His car, wallet, everything he owned, left behind. Not to mention the fact that he left without a word...to any of us. I felt sick as I stared at the flier I brought back from the library the day he disappeared. It hung from the bulletin board, amongst others offering typing, dog walking, and just about any other service imaginable. *The crazy alien-professor guy, coming to speak at our college? This can't be good.* I planned on showing it to Joshua as soon as I got home. Now there it was, on the coffee table in front of us, unknown to Joshua and irrelevant.

That damn professor! He thinks he knows so much about aliens? This can't be a coincidence. His upcoming speech at the university must have something to do with all of this, even if Cole and Mani don't believe it.

Patricia Miller

I'm so dumb, refusing to tell him how much I loved him. I would give anything to have him here, with me. I cringed, thinking I might not ever get the chance to tell him now. *It's all got to be my way, huh? Take things slow. Be friends and see where it goes. Stupid. Stupid!*

As if waiting would change the fact that he's an alien. Alien or human, it didn't matter. So what...I loved an alien. It's not like I've ever felt this way about any human I've ever known.

I've never dated anyone like him. No one, none of my boyfriends, ever came close to him. No one got me the way he did. I mean, does. Quit talking like he's dead, Emma. I'm never taking him for granted again. I swallowed hard, dragged out of my personal pity party by Cole:

"We need to call the police," he said.

Mani shot a disdainful glance in his direction. "Oh yeah, alien," he said. "Guess we can't do that."

"Yeah," said Mani. "No police."

"I can't stand this," I said, cradling my throbbing head in my hands. "I just can't stand sitting here, doing nothing."

"Well, what can we do?" asked Cole. He paced back and forth in front of me.

"Who would want to hurt him?" asked Mani.

How can she sit there, all calm-like, talking? Was this was part of the new, improved, mature Mani? "Is there anyone that hates him enough to kidnap him?" she continued.

"I can't think of anyone who hates him at all," I said.

Mani smiled and snickered under her breath. "I can think of someone who used to hate him...hate him pretty badly, in fact."

Cole and I sat in silence, looking at her. I knew who, and I think Cole knew, too. Mani herself. The person who now felt blessed by the chance she got to come to Earth. The person who stowed away on Josh's craft, and later almost died if not for his unrelenting care. Or alien, that is.

"I hated him, *really* hated him." She continued, locked into a daydreamer's stare, shaking her head in disgust. "I was so immature, so ungrateful."

"Hate's an ugly thing," Cole said. His voice, low and stern. The glare in his eyes, eerie. "Hate's pretty scary."

Mani snickered again, apparently trying to lighten the feeling in the room. "Yeah, well I'm glad I don't feel that way anymore."

All became silent once again. I felt a hot flush spreading over my skin. I sat still, though. Confused. Thinking. *What's going on in me? I am worried about Joshua. Mani and Cole are, too. But, I'm definitely feeling something else, something different. Could it have something to do with what Mani was saying?*

"My eyes have been opened by him for good," she said now, smiling. "He has such a wonderfully sweet soul. Josha has taught me that I couldn't go on hating anymore." Mani paused and looked from one of us to the other. "Life is fragile, you know? Any of us could be gone tomorrow, today even. His friendship is something very special. I intend to treasure it for the rest of my life."

The next thing I knew, my nails were digging into the cushion. *What the heck is up with her? Talk about weirdo crazy! Has she lost her mind? She's talking awful sweet about the guy I love. And she's with Cole!*

Cole stared at me as I felt the furrows in my forehead deepening. *I'm not jealous. Don't look at me like you think I'm jealous. I'm not jealous.*

I quickly stood, turning away and toward the window, giving myself time to get it together. Once I did, an interesting thought came into my mind: *That's it. That's it. Could that be it...the answer?*

I spun to face the two of them again.

55

EMMA

"Mani, did you talk to anyone about your feelings...you know...about how you hated Josh?"

I will not call him Josha. He's Joshua or Josh, to me. I peered at her, trying to squash down my jealousy. *So what? She cares for him. She's always going to care for him. It's not like it's going to threaten my relationship with him. Right?*

"Well," she answered. "I never told anyone that we were aliens, of course. But, yes, I did complain to Rick about how I thought Josha had...sort of...thrown me away."

"What did he say? How did he act when you told him?"

I looked at Cole. He looked back at me. *We're thinking the same thing: Rick could be responsible for all of this!*

He stood and gently grabbed Mani's arms just below her shoulders, facing her, staring directly into her eyes. "This is important, Mani. Rick could be the one who has Josh."

"Well, he *did* say how awful it was that Josha had hurt me," Mani admitted. "I laid it on pretty thick." She crinkled her nose, but no tears came.

"It could be Rick," Cole shouted in my direction.

Our plans formed quickly. Mani called Rick to arrange an informal lunch date. Then, per Cole's suggestion, we would follow him from a distance.

They discussed the plans. I heard their words. But they were just words. As weightless as air.

I stood up and walked to the window. I gazed out, but instead of trees, I saw Josh. *He's being held, maybe chained up. Maybe...may-be...hurt.* Before I knew it, tears slid down my cheeks, onto my top. I felt a hand on my shoulder. Cole.

"He'll be OK, Emma," Cole whispered. His breath, so soft against my ear. I turned to him. His thumb brushed the tears from my face. "I know you're scared. We all are, but we'll find him. He'll be all right."

How can he be so sure, so calm? I can't be that sure...of anything. All I could manage was a nod. I turned around and stared back out at the street, letting my eyes wander to the porch and the swing. Josh and I had sat there together a lot before he disappeared. It was...our place.

Cole, meanwhile, was acting kinda weird, the way he looked and talked to me. *Yeah, we're all friends, the four of us. But, doesn't he realize how I feel about Josh? Doesn't he know?* My heart hurt so badly with him gone. My hands felt cold, then hot, then cold again. Whole body felt restless, and I struggled to hide a constant trembling, all over, inside. I tried wrapping my arms around my torso, but I couldn't stop the quivering, no matter what.

Cole and Mani finished the plans to follow Rick the next day. *Tomorrow? How could we wait till tomorrow? How could I wait till tomorrow?* I had to find him, wrap my arms around him, kiss him hard and tell him I never wanted to be without him, ever again. *What if we don't find him? No, you can't think that way!*

I turned back, this time really listening to them. Afterward, Mani went to the bathroom to shower. I sat on a chair, staring out onto the porch. Cole made a bed for himself on the couch with some sheets Mani had given him. *That's right! I didn't think! Mani just told him the truth about her and Josh. I wonder how he's taking the news.*

I looked over at him. "I'm sure it wasn't easy, finding out your girlfriend...is an alien." I watched his face. He smiled. *Is he trying to act like it's no big deal?*

"I'll admit, it was...kinda tough to swallow at first," he answered. "But, Mani explained it well. It's sort of...wild...hard to believe. But, it explains a lot about Josh."

"Did she show you her secret powers?"

"You could say that." He paused, then continued: "You know how it feels. You went through the same thing. Didn't you?"

"I guess so," I answered. "It all seemed a much bigger deal before." I thought before I said more. "It felt like something I couldn't deal with. But now, it seems like it's nothing at all. It's so strange."

"You had trouble handling it?" he asked.

"Oh yeah," I said. "It's not like it's a small thing, like a different religion or ethnicity or something."

"You call those small things?" he said. "Those are often reasons for breakups."

"Well, if you ask me, they're stupid reasons. They're nothing compared to being from a different planet."

"Oh, I don't know." Cole was now finished with his bed; he sat on the chair catty corner from me. "Being from a different planet is the same as a different culture. I can see why it might not work out."

"But, you seem so calm about Mani being an alien," I explained. "You act like it's no problem for you."

"Now you're making assumptions and jumping to conclusions, Emma. Calm? No. But, I love her," he explained. "I'm still working all of it out in my mind. In all honesty, I am having some trouble wrapping my brain around it."

"I think Mani thinks you're all right with everything," I said.

"I didn't say I'm not," he insisted. "There's no reason to go worrying Mani, right now. But I need more time to think about it."

I nodded. *I don't buy his calm act. And I don't want to see Mani hurt. But, I have my own stuff to deal with right now.* I felt ashamed of being jealous of Mani, of her "special relationship" with "Josha." *Why do I hate it when she calls him Josha? It was his given name back on Theos.*

He belonged to another world, filled with beings like him. Like Mani.

I drifted into Joshua's room, fell onto his bed, and pulled the sheets up to my face. *His smell.* Mercifully, I fell asleep, engulfed in loneliness and tears.

The next day, Mani met Rick for lunch at a nearby café. Cole and I watched from a distance in the car. Cole had a pair of binoculars up to his eyes, aimed in the direction of their outdoor table. I didn't bring it up, but I couldn't help but think about our conversation from the night before. He didn't fool me, though. This alien thing was really freaking him out. He wasn't sure about his relationship with Mani. And it made me realize how confused I felt about Joshua and I. Being in a relationship with an Earthling wouldn't cause such problems. Yeah...that would be a lot easier.

My thoughts drifted to the brief fling I'd had with Cole. He was sweet, but I didn't feel the connection with him I felt with Joshua. Sure, I just *had* to feel a deep connection with an alien. Just my rotten luck. I looked over at Cole, remembering his gentle and loving touch. He *did* actually have a beautiful smile. And just look at those adorable dimples, and rock hard body. I turned abruptly away. *What am I doing? First I need to be friends with Joshua. Then, I realize my deep love for him and can't wait to tell him. Then, I ponder the sweetness of a relationship with Cole, my friend's boyfriend. Why should any guy bother with someone as messed up as me?*

"Cole," I said, breaking open my own trance. "I've been thinking about what you said last night."

"Yeah?"

"Well, I was wondering...Have you thought about how much easier it would be to just find someone from Earth to be with, rather than an alien?"

"Of course," he said, without a moment's thought. "That's what I meant. I don't know if I can handle this...being with an alien." He paused, looked away from his binoculars, and then looked back into them. "Why?" He blinked. "I assume you're thinking that?"

"I guess so," I said. "I mean...it *has* crossed my mind. Anyway, Joshua and I are just friends."

"You know, you and I weren't together very long, but it sure was nice."

I nodded, then we both kept watching the lunch date. He shifted slightly in his seat. *Did he just inch a little closer to me? It feels like he did. No, I'm just imagining it.* Before too long, Mani was back in the car with us and we were on our way, tracking Rick from a distance.

"I'm certain it's Rick," Mani said, clicking her seat-belt into place. "He was flirting and talking about us...as if there was an 'us'."

"Maybe he thought there was," I said.

"I never did anything to make him think so," she insisted.

"He probably came to that conclusion on his own," said Cole, keeping his speed low, and staying a few cars behind Rick.

"Anyway, I feel certain it's Rick," Mani repeated. We followed him back to his apartment, then stayed out there, sitting and watching, for over an hour, until finally Cole decided to go back home.

"We're not going to find out anything tonight."

At home, we got a message from the library.

"Why didn't we think about work? I emailed all his Profs and got him excused for a family emergency. How could I forget about work?" I said.

"We have to do something. What should we do?" asked Mani.

"I know," said Cole. "We'll send an email from his email saying that he got called away. We'll say…his mom is sick."

"Do you think we should?" I asked.

"What else *can* we do?" asked Cole.

Cole logged into Josh's computer. *How did he know his password? That's interesting.*

"We can go back to Rick's apartment after dark." Cole turned to Mani. "If you get a feeling…you know…that feeling you guys get…then we'll know Josh is nearby."

56

TRACKING

Cole and Mani snuggled on the couch, waiting for it to get dark. I decided to get out of the house, choosing to sit on the front porch steps. *I'm not sitting on that swing without Josh. I don't even want to look at it.* The breeze was cool and it gently lifted my hair. I leaned my head against the railing, trying to let the evening air comfort me.

Soon, I opened my eyes to the sight of Cole and Mani standing above me. Cole dangled his jeep keys in his left hand while Mani gently pulled him toward the car by his right. I took a deep breath and rose to my feet. Walking in the same direction, I looked up at the sky, as if to pray for Joshua's safe return. *I wonder if I'm looking towards Theos. Which direction is it?* His planet seemed as much a mystery as Heaven itself.

The drive felt long, particularly on account of its silence. *So, what exactly will we do if Mani senses Josh? We don't have guns. Mani is the strongest weapon we have. I wonder if Cole realizes that.* I reached into my jacket pocket and pulled out my can of mace. Joshua had asked me to carry it at night. At the time, I thought his concern was cute. Now I held the can tightly, smiling over how non-cute it had been...

We stopped about a block from Rick's apartment complex. Mani was in charge now, as she was the one most familiar with the area.

"OK, we walk from here," she instructed. "Stay out of the street lights."

We nodded and piled out of the jeep. Cole and I followed Mani into someone's backyard, then quietly made our way toward the building. I walked in between Mani and Cole, feeling safer in the middle.

The street lights cast an eerie glow onto the blacktop. I shuddered as the chill of the night air touched me. *Am I cold or scared? Probably both.* Cole put his hand on my shoulder. *Funny, that actually made me feel a little calmer.* We stopped behind our leader and stood in the shadow of some tall, thick bushes along the side of the apartment building. Mani put up one finger to tell us to give her a minute, and so we waited. Then she turned and signaled for us to cross another small area of grass. When we arrived at the other side, in the shadow of another row of bushes, Mani became as still as stone.

"What is it?" I whispered.

She didn't immediately reply. After a moment, she turned her head and spoke.

"I can barely sense him," she said. "It's weak, but I'm sure it's him. It has to be."

"Why isn't it strong?" Cole asked.

"I don't know," Mani answered. "Maybe he was here, but isn't now. Or maybe he's at a distance from here."

"Well," Cole said sternly. "Any sense, strong or light, means Rick is the guilty party."

"Hold on," I insisted. "Don't get carried away."

"Cole," said Mani. "I want to find him as much and as soon as you do, but let's not jump the gun. Let's move in a little closer."

"We don't want to get caught," I reminded her.

"I'll just move in closer by myself then," said Mani. "That way I can still tell if I sense him and we'll have less of a chance of getting caught."

"I don't like that," said Cole.

He's protecting her.

"I can take care of myself, Cole," she insisted, and I believed her. Without waiting for a reply, much less permission, Mani moved in closer, and it didn't take long for her to return with a report.

"It's the same minute trace as I felt here," she explained. "It's not enough to move on, but at least we know Joshua was in the vicinity, and not that long ago."

Cole argued with us about it, but Mani and I agreed that we needed to return home and come up with a plan of attack to fool Rick into caving in. Cole disagreed with the whole thing, but he himself caved after Mani gave him...well, a look. That's pretty much all it took.

I saw where Cole was coming from, though. *I want to find him, too, but I don't want to be stupid about it. If we confront Rick now and don't find Josh, we might ruin any chance we have of finding him.*

The next morning I awoke to a strange sound.

Mani was screaming at Cole. *Loud.* I grabbed my robe and made my way into the kitchen.

57

FINDING

"I can't believe you," Mani yelled at Cole. "What were you thinking?"

"What's wrong?" I asked, rubbing my watery eyes.

"Nothing's wrong," Cole answered. "In fact everything's right now."

"Right?" yelled Mani. "You call driving over to Rick's apartment and shoving him into a wall right?!"

"Cole," I said. "You didn't..."

"I did," he said, eyes bugging out. "I did, and I'm glad I did."

I sighed. *This is out of control. Where's the coffee?*

"Listen," he continued. "I got him to confess, Emma. I think I know where Josh is."

Lowering the cup from my mouth, I gazed from Mani to Cole and back again. *Could this be true? If so, why are they wasting time fighting about this?* I ran to Joshua's room, threw on jeans and a t-shirt, and then ran back out into the kitchen. I sat on a chair, bending down to slip on my shoes.

"You agreed we should wait 'til today to do anything," Mani yelled. "You said—"

"What are you doing?" Cole asked me, interrupting Mani's fury.

"You're either going to tell me where he is or you're both going to shut up and come with me." *I don't plan on arguing about this crap with either of them. If they don't shut up and come, I'm leaving without them.*

They both grabbed their shoes and jackets in silence, and before long, once again I found myself sitting in the back seat of Cole's jeep. The sun glared in my eyes, my watering eyes. Vaguely, I became aware I was picking the skin around my nails. *Josh. Josh.*

I didn't know where we were going, nor did I care. I didn't know what we'd do when we got there, but once again, I didn't care. The only thing on my mind was seeing Joshua, safe and by my side. Cole barely stopped at the 4-way signs, and I soon realized we were in a section of town that was totally unfamiliar to me. He pulled the car onto one side of the street and shifted the gear into park.

Sighing, Cole said, "Rick said he locked him in a cellar in an old, abandoned house."

I struggled to hear every word Cole said. That and to stop picking my fingers, which were threatening to bleed.

"I think it's that one, over there." He pointed to a two-story home, dark siding, maybe charcoal or gray. He explained that no one was guarding Joshua, and that he'd scared Rick so bad that "We didn't have to worry about him interfering."

"How do we know he's telling the truth?" asked Mani. "There could be *several* men guarding him for all we know."

"I'm sure he told the truth," insisted Cole. "I'm pretty sure I scared the piss out of him, maybe even literally."

Cole sounded ridiculously sure. Emphasis on ridiculously. Sure, Rick didn't seem real manly to me—manipulative, maybe. But he wasn't stupid.

There we sat, in front of Joshua's presumed three-day prison. As I stared at the two-story structure, made of brick with paint chipping from its trim, my heart raced. I prepared myself to see him again.

Is he here? Is he alive? Could I really be getting him back?

58

RESCUING

"You two better wait here," said Cole. He searched his trunk for tools; metal clanked all around. I opened my door, but hesitated, my leg dangling on the outside, shoe barely grazing the pavement.

"Fine by me," Mani answered, not moving from the passenger seat.

"Not fine by me," I retorted. Now out of the back seat, I stood facing him.

He slammed the trunk, grasping a crow bar. *Oh, red face. He's perturbed. Too bad for him.*

"I have no idea what I'm going to find in there," he warned. I saw he was also clutching some other long, metal object. Didn't know what it was, but I assumed he planned to use it for self-defense, if necessary.

"Exactly my point," I answered. "You might need help."

He sighed. "Emma, he might look awful, like— scary. And I'm sure he wouldn't want me to put you in any danger."

Mmm, I can see his point there. Assuming Joshua was alive, as I refused to believe anything else, he *would* want me kept from danger. *But Cole doesn't have to know I get that.* "He's coming home in the car with us, so I'll have to see him eventually. Besides," I argued, "you said that Rick didn't have anyone guarding him, so where's the danger?"

Cole stepped closer to me, our faces only inches apart. His breath touched my face as he sighed again. "I don't want you in there."

He looked stern, but somehow a gentleness emerged from his eyes. I felt the heaviness of his stare, the close proximity of his body. And although I didn't know the reason, I felt uncomfortable, so I nonchalantly took a step backwards, hoping he wouldn't notice. "OK, maybe you're right. I'll stay here with Mani. But will you at least text or call me as soon as you see how he is?"

Cole stepped away and walked in the direction of the back door. Finally, he agreed to my demands by raising his hand and nodding.

I stayed outside the car, too restless to sit. Leaned against Mani's side; her window was down. Purposefully, I didn't start a conversation with her. I just didn't feel like talking, and Cole's strange behavior was cluttering my mind. Disturbing me, actually. But then again, so was this whole situation. Thankfully, she didn't say a word. Good. I needed to think.

We waited for what felt forever. I paced back and forth between the house and car. I practically jumped when my cell phone rang, answering it almost immediately. Mani looked up in my direction, listening.

"Yeah," I said shortly. *It's hard to breathe. Breathe. Breathe, you stupid lungs.*

"He's all right Emma," Cole said calmly. "He's dirty and exhausted, but he's not hurt."

I sighed so deep I swore my lungs would collapse. Tears filled my eyes, then slipped down my cheeks. I wiped them away, asking if I should come and help.

"No, I don't think so," he said. "I'm gonna bring him to the car in a minute."

He hung up. No goodbye. I went back to pacing 'til Cole finally came out the back door, with Joshua's arm over his shoulder. Josh was clearly worn-out and weak, trying to keep up with Cole's pace. When he looked up, I saw him try to straighten up and carry his own weight a bit more. I smiled so wide my face muscles felt pinched. As for Mani, she jumped out of the car. I got on the other side of Josh to help, but he insisted he was fine. I let go.

Cole sat him in the back seat, leaving the door open for some air. Just as well, since Joshua's feet were on the outside of the car. He rested back on the seat in a sideways position. Once he seemed to catch his breath, I stepped toward him. Crouching down, I looked into his face. Despite all of my plans about telling him my feelings, I came up empty. All I could do was smile. More tears slid down over my cheeks.

"Thank God you're safe," I said. I laid my hand on his, which itself sat lifelessly upon his lap, skin and fingernails caked with dirt.

He raised his head and smiled at me. His face was also dirty, and he smelled of mold and mildew, but to me, he was the best sight imaginable. When our eyes met, I thought I noticed...glassiness. Abruptly, his head dropped. He seemed to lean a bit in my direction, and I instinctively leaned forward and wrapped my arms around him, holding him. As he broke the embrace, he wiped his face with his hands, looked at me, and spoke.

59

EMMA

"Thank you...for not giving up on me," he whispered.

"We...I...could never do that," I answered. My eyes, glued to his, wide, glistening (both of ours). My breathing, locked, imprisoned in the rhythm of his. *Tell him? Now? Or, maybe later. No, now. I should.*

Cole broke our trance. "Let's get him back to the cabin."

I jumped in back beside Josh. Mani and Cole rode in front. As we drove, I remembered a bottle of water in my purse. I pulled it out; Josh downed it. He spent a great deal of time staring out the window, his head back, resting against the seat, eyes closed, quiet, pensive.

Back at the house, Joshua wasted no time taking a shower.

"Look," Cole said to Mani and me while Josh was in the bathroom. "I think we should hold off on asking too many questions."

"What do you mean?" Mani asked.

"Hold off on questions. Don't push."

Who died and left you in charge?

Josh said he had some meals while locked up, yet he scarfed and stuffed food into his face, nonstop. Once finished, he immediately walked onto the porch and sat on the swing. I started in that direction, only to be stopped by Cole. His hand snaked around my arm.

"Maybe we should let him alone," he said. I looked at Josh, sitting on the swing, staring off blankly. *What is he thinking? I want to be beside him, comforting him, telling him...*

"Maybe he wants some friendly company," I answered.

I broke away from Cole's grip and walked slowly through the front door, each step heavy, porch wood squeaking beneath. Surprisingly, Josh didn't move. Squeak after squeak. No movement. Not a twitch. I stopped, stood in front of him.

"Can I join you?" I asked gently.

"I wouldn't be good company right now," he said, eyes still far away.

So, do I...leave? Stay? What? I stood there frozen.

"We don't have to talk," I said. "We can just...sit."

He didn't say a word. Just nodded in agreement. I sat down beside him. Silence. And more silence. Awkward and weird. Finally, he spoke...

"I thought I'd go crazy in that cellar," he said. "I couldn't have stood it much longer."

"I wish we found you sooner."

"It was a long three days," he said, and then he was silent for the next 15 minutes, at least. *I love you. I need to tell you that. And that I can't live without you. If you were gone, I know I'd have wanted to die. You can't leave my life. You have to be in my life. I love you. Why don't I speak? Tell him!*

"It was a long three days without you," I said, without turning my head in his direction. He was silent for what seemed an eternity. What was he thinking? Should I have waited to tell him? The silence was killing me. And then I felt his hand on my leg.

And I instinctively laid mine on top of his.

I should have told him more. But I didn't. I wasn't sure if it was the right thing to lay on him so soon after his return. My feelings hadn't changed, but my certainty in communicating them had wavered. I just couldn't seem to get past my fear. What I feared above all was his response.

"I'm tired," he said. "It will feel so good to sleep on a real bed again."

I nodded. He got up and went into the house, and directly into his room, shutting the door behind him. I followed him inside and walked into the kitchen, where Mani and Cole sat talking. They were leaning over something on the table. Mani eyed me with concern.

I pulled a soda out of the fridge and joined them at the table. "What's this?" I asked, looking down at a notebook. Cole closed it and looked in my direction.

"Well, it's a notebook that Rick used to communicate with Josh while he was locked in the cellar." I heard his words, but they didn't take hold inside my mind.

"Communicate?" I asked. "How did he do that? Why would he do that?"

"I don't know yet how, but it seems he wanted to tell Josh some things," Cole explained. Mani kept quiet, looking from one of us to the other. "Josh wrote a few things back. But he doesn't know it was Rick yet, and he doesn't know that we know it was Rick. I'm not sure if he should ever know."

"I think he has a right to know eventually," I said.

Then Mani spoke for the first time since I'd entered:

"That's what I told him," she said.

"Well, maybe in time." Cole got up and started to walk away from the table, carrying the notebook with him.

"Hey," I demanded. "Where do you think you're going with that?"

He stopped and turned toward me. "It's just a bunch of ridiculous ramblings. I grabbed it from the cellar and stuck it inside my jacket. Josh doesn't even know I have it."

"If you've read it, I can, too," I insisted.

"I didn't read it all," said Mani. "He wouldn't let me."

"Like I told Mani," he explained. "I think it should be given to Josh, for him to do with as he pleases. After all, it is his personal writing."

I thought about it for a minute...and it did seem the most decent thing to do. But I still thought it was wrong that Cole had read it. I wondered why he hadn't left it in the cellar, or given it directly to Josh. I then realized it was entirely possible that Josh had asked him to take it. But he hadn't asked about it yet.

"I say we give it to Josh immediately," I said.

"As soon as he gets up," said Cole.

"And between now and then," I said. "We will keep it in the safe."

I knew the combination, and used it quickly. Cole didn't argue. He handed it to me and both of them watched me lock it in.

60

HEALING

Cole was giving off some really weird vibes, and for that reason I preferred to avoid him for the time being. The front porch swing felt the best to me. As I sat there, thoughts zoomed in and out of my mind. *He must have been terrified. Cold. Scared. Alone. You love him. Why didn't you tell him? What's he thinking now? Does he care? If he did, why didn't he tell me? Maybe he doesn't. Maybe I'm alone in my feelings.*

My thoughts became...heavy. My weak, tired mind buckled under their pressure. I allowed my body to lower onto a pillow on the swing. Rest. *Rest.* Sleep came easily.

The next thing I knew, I awoke to the afternoon sun peeking through the limbs of the large, front yard tree. My mind, as well as my body, was no longer tired, but sharp. Alert. Strong. Refreshed. A growl from my stomach was a cue to eat supper. I sat up and rubbed my eyes before making my way into the kitchen.

A distinct aroma filled the air: chicken. As Mani stirred noodles, I bent down to peer into the oven door window, through which I saw thighs sizzling on a cookie sheet. She set plates on the table, and I reached into the silverware drawer to help. When I turned toward the table, spoons and forks in hand, I found Mani staring at me.

"What?" I asked. "I'm sorry I fell asleep. I would have helped with dinner if you would have called me."

"Oh, that's OK," she said, breaking the stare and continuing to tend to the table.

"So..." I said. "Is there something wrong?"

"No." The word came out short and quick.

I knew her better than that. Something was up, so I stopped and stared at her until she broke. "Well, Josh has the notebook."

"Cole gave it to him?" I asked.

"Yeah," she said. "He's in his room with it now."

We finished setting the table and sat down on either side, waiting for the timer to ring. I was engrossed in my thoughts of how Josh must have felt, reading those sick communications between him and Rick. I also thought about Rick, about how angry I was that he wouldn't get his due. But Joshua couldn't turn him in. It would draw too much attention to him and Mani. Their secret had to remain as such, no matter what.

My cell phone rang and, seeing that it was my little sister, I stepped out of the room into the privacy of the dining room.

"Hey, Hope," I answered.

"Hi sis."

"What's up?"

"Ha. Can't a girl just call her sister without needing a reason?" she asked, with no small amount of attitude.

"Sure they can, if they're some other girl's sister," I laughed.

"Come on," she protested. Then: "OK, I do have a reason."

"I knew it. Spill it."

"Well, it's boy stuff," she explained. "I could use an ear and maybe some advice."

"We're due for a lunch together," I said. "Let's meet. How about tomorrow?"

"Cool," she said, letting out a sigh.

All of us, including Josh, ate at the table. No one brought up the notebook, and Josh was pretty quiet and sullen. After he was done eating, he asked if anyone would mind if he went straight back to bed. Of course no one did, and that was all I saw of him that night. After helping Cole and Mani with the dishes, I left for my own place for the night.

61

EMMA

The next day, my sister and I met at her favorite fast food restaurant. I managed to avoid the grease by ordering a salad. She wore an outfit only she could pull off. *How does she wear so many different colors and still look cute? I'd look a fool, that's for sure.*

She sipped her milkshake, crossing and uncrossing her pencil thin legs beneath the table as she spoke:

"You wouldn't even believe my life, right now." She rolled her eyes.

"Oh, yeah?" I asked. "The way mine's been going, try me."

"So, there's this guy. He's from a different school, and he's so cool," she explained. Her idea of cool, as I understood it, was someone who spoke, dressed, and acted in weird, mysterious ways. She went on to describe him, and confirmed just that.

"Sounds like he's trying way too hard to be cool," I said when she was done.

"You don't even know him," she insisted.

"No," I said. "But from what you tell me, I get the overall picture."

"That's *not* fair," she squealed.

"What's not fair about it?" I asked. "I'm not making anything up. I'm just going by what you say."

She took a deep breath and sighed. "So you really think that, huh?"

As I was beginning to answer her, she looked away and smiled in a very flirtatious manner at a teenage boy who was carrying his tray to a table, to sit with a man who appeared to be his dad. His had dark hair, falling barely above his eyes, which were similar in color to the boy's. He seemed pleased by Hope's attention, and raised his free hand, waving back at her.

"Who's that?" I asked.

"Oh, that's my bud, Jordan," she said, not taking her eyes off him.

"Is that the guy you were telling me about?" I asked.

She jerked her head back in my direction, a furrow set deep between her eyes. "No, that's not him."

"Oh. Well, he seems nice," I observed.

"Yeah, he's real nice," she answered. "He's my bud."

At that moment, the young man made his way over to our table. Hope got up and met him halfway. I was inclined to think she didn't want me to hear their conversation. In any case, I did watch the two of them from the corners of my eyes. It was clear they had a special friendship. Maybe more, especially on his part. He never took his eyes off of her, and his body remained unusually close for *just a friend.* Nor could he hide the flush of red in his cheeks. Soon they said their goodbyes and parted. She sat back down, staring at me, reading the look on my face, which I made no attempt to hide.

"What?" she demanded.

"You know what," I insisted, grinning.

"We're just friends," she insisted again.

"Now, that's the way a boy should treat you..." I offered.

I spent the next several minutes explaining the difference between the two boys' characters. She winced several times, but I knew she understood me. At least she didn't get mad and storm out of the place. I finished off with a dose of "trust me, I've been there" and "every girl makes the mistake of choosing the boy who seems cool and dangerous." Her eyes widened. *Maybe I'm getting through.*

I dropped her at home before driving back to the cabin. I couldn't help but consider the advice I'd given her. I recalled my words to her: "Sometimes the best guy for us is right under our noses, and we don't give them the proper chance." *Pretty good advice, Emma. So, how many times did I make that same mistake? It's so much easier to give advice than take it.*

I pulled up Josh's drive half in a daze, still thinking of my conversation with Sis, when I saw him sitting on the front porch swing. His blank face sickened me, an empty shell of a man. *OK, Emma, enough messin' around.* I at last made my decision.

I have to tell him my feelings. Right now. Do it! Just do it!

I felt strong, jumping out of the car, slamming the door shut with resolve. I walked up the walk, fast as I could without running, skipping steps up onto the porch. As I stopped in front of him, his head lifted.

A glistening, a *gleam*, shone from his eyes. His lips moved slightly, giving the impression that a smile might emerge, but I guess it never found its way to the surface.

Was that gleam meant for me? Is he ready to hear this?

62

EMMA

"Have a seat," he said, looking at me, really *looking at me* for the first time since he'd returned. I sat, feeling this warmth coming from his body. We turned and faced each other, smiled, then looked away again.

"How are you feeling?" I asked.

"Better." His voice was smooth; words flowed effortlessly now. "How was lunch with your sister?"

"Nice," I said. "She wanted to talk about boys." I laughed a little.

"Boys, huh?" he said. Then, after a pause: "We males require a meeting to discuss?"

"Sometimes," I said. "She has a lot to learn about picking the right guy, but who am I kidding? So do I."

"Oh, come on," he said. "I'm sure you had good advice for her."

"Yeah, advice on what *not* to do," I answered. My turn to pause. Then: "Ever stop and think about your own choices?"

"Sure, I have," he said. He seemed distracted, heavy in thought. "Emma, that time...down in...that cellar. It made me...think...really think, about my life and the people in it."

"Did it?" I asked. *Did that sound as dumb as I think it did? He doesn't seem to think so...*

"Yeah." His face, stern and sullen. "I didn't know what was going on, or why I was being held there, or even if I'd get out alive."

I swallowed hard. *Not sure I can take hearing this. But I should let him talk.*

"And when he started to write to me in that notebook...It made me take a good look at myself, the way I've been acting. My future."

He took a deep breath and leaned over, cradling his head in both hands. I draped my arm across his back, trying to comfort him. His back rose and fell with another breath. Then he sat back up, his leg grazing the side of mine. After a moment, he continued:

"My being from another planet...is so unfair to you. I try to be normal...like humans, but no matter how good I get at pretending, I will never be a human," he sighed.

"Who says you have to be human?" I asked. "I never said I needed you to be human."

"But, you *deserve* a human," he explained. "You shouldn't have to deal with my problems."

"Your problems?" I asked. "Do you think being from Theos instead of Earth is a problem?"

"Isn't it?" he asked.

"No," I said. "I think it's cool."

"Cool?" he said in exasperation. "I have to hide who I really am, all of the time. I'm alone. No family, and I have to always make sure no one sees me doing...you know...things humans can't do."

"So?" I said.

"So?" he said back. "I'd call that problems. It certainly isn't a dream boyfriend."

"Says you!" I found myself almost shouting. "What do you know about dream boyfriends?"

We both paused for a shared deep breath. We each sat back on the swing. Silence. I heard him breathing. That, and the squeaking of the porch swing chains.

Don't cry. Don't cry. This isn't going right. How do I fix this?

"I'm sorry," he said, pausing slightly before continuing. "I didn't mean to make you mad."

"I know," I answered. "Like I said, what do you know about a dream boyfriend?"

"I don't," he said. "But I feel fairly certain it's not me."

That's it. No more playing around. "Explain. Why isn't it you?" *Stay calm.*

He stared at me. *What is that look? He seems impatient. Don't get...mad...at me...*

"Come on, Emma." His tone was gentle and soft. "You know how I feel about you, how I've always felt about you. The only reason I ever questioned us was because of my being an alien, and the problems that go along with that. You deserve a normal life, with a normal guy."

He's opening up. Should I say something? I don't know what to say. What do I say?

He interrupted my stream of thoughts: "The only thing that hurt worse than letting you go was seeing you with Cole." He froze, suddenly seeming thoughtful. "And you are the only thing that kept me sane in that cellar."

I looked straight into his eyes as he spoke. *Is this happening? Is he really saying this?*

"I didn't know *when* or *if* I'd ever get out. But if I thought of you...our friendship...I had that hope to hold onto."

He looked away abruptly, staring out into the street again, just like when he'd first come back. Empty. Almost paralyzed.

I sat quietly, reeling from all he'd said. Trying to decide where to take this.

No more excuses. It's time to own up.

To everything.

63

REVEALING

What did she just say? Am I asleep? She's really saying it?

"Joshua. Are you listening to me? Are you all right?"

There we sat, our legs still slightly touching. *What's wrong with me? Am I...I'm shaking. She said it. She just looked at me...and said it. She did, didn't she? Maybe I just imagined it. I can't say it back, if she didn't really say it.* "Did Cole tell you about the notebook?"

"Yes."

"I'm going to burn it."

"Why?" she asked.

"Why?" I echoed. "Why would I want it?"

She nodded. Enough said.

"The last time you and I spoke about us, we had decided it best to just be friends and see where it takes us," I said.

"Yes," she replied. "That is what we said."

I stood, walked over to the railing, then turned and leaned my weight onto it, facing her. "I just want what's best for you. I made a promise to myself when I came to this planet."

"What promise?" she asked.

"Look at all I've done to you in such a short time. I've hurt you. I've lied to you. I've loved you and left you." *Did I just say that??* "And I got you all mixed up in danger." I slapped my thighs. "I'm so much trouble, Emma."

"I don't see you as trouble," she said.

"Listen to yourself," I argued. "You talk about your little sister, Hope. You want her to make good decisions about guys. Would you tell her *I* would be a good decision to be in a relationship with if she was in your place?"

She hesitated before answering. "I might have told her not to choose you initially, but I would be wrong."

"What you really mean is you would tell her to turn and run, *fast*." I turned away from her and gazed up at the sun, which was now lowering, and about to hide behind some trees in the distance.

"Maybe," she said. "But I also said I'd be wrong. Listen, I might have some good advice for her at times, but today...today I realized *she* taught *me* a lesson."

"What's that?" I asked, turning back toward her.

"That sometimes, we don't realize the right person is right under our noses, and that we don't give them the chance they deserve."

"You said that?" I couldn't help it; I grinned.

"Yes," she said. "Maybe...we...us..." She was now standing, facing me.

I slipped my hand around hers. Stunned at how good it felt. A surge of energy struck me from inside; goose bumps covered my skin. *My back is glowing. I just know it!*

"I don't care that you are an alien. In fact, I'm a little tired of hearing about what a big deal it is," she whispered.

"What?"

"OK. You're different. I get all of that. That doesn't change the fact that I can't stop thinking about you. The whole time I was with Cole, I wasn't really *with* him. My mind...my heart was with you. Not only can I cope with all your oddities, I can't live without them." She stepped over to the railing beside me, looking out into the night.

I stepped in closer to her, dangerously close. I then curled behind her and rested my hands on the hips of her jeans. Her body, warm and comforting.

Finally, lowering my mouth to her ear, I exhaled, making her shiver. "Turn around Emma."

She took a deep breath. Her feet pivoted. She faced me. *I always knew she was beautiful, but...wow!*

64

BEGINNING

The evening drew down on the four of us. We sat around a campfire outside the cabin. I stared into the golden flames, understanding how a moth must feel: drawn in. My fingers trembled, clutching the notebook from my time in the cellar. The trembling wasn't from the chill. It wasn't cold out there, around the fire. Cole tended to the embers, poking them with a tree limb.

"Josh. Josh..." Mani called to me.

I looked her way, trying to focus my eyes through the smoke. "What?"

"I'm going in for a drink. Do you want anything?"

"Oh." My eyes got drawn right back to the fire. "No."

Mani walked inside and came back out quickly, returning to her spot beside Cole. Cole looked lonely while she was gone, even for those few moments. *I know they've been talking this whole time. Wonder what I missed.*

"So..." Cole looked at me. "You've decided to burn it, huh?"

I looked at him as he nodded down at the notebook, still clenched between my trembling hands.

"Might as well. It's nothing but a crazy man's ramblings." Yet still, the notebook was in one piece.

"I don't blame you, Josh." Mani's voice carried a soft sense of reassurance. "It's over. Best to burn it and move on."

"Don't rush him," Emma chimed in, her voice equally nurturing, supportive. "Take your time. Do whatever you want."

"I'm just glad I leaned on Rick. I couldn't wait any longer," Cole explained.

"I would have ferreted it out of him, if you would have given me more time," Mani noted, apparently still annoyed about Cole taking the situation into his own hands.

Cole shook his head, said, "That night...you know...the night we followed him home and you said you sensed Josh? I decided right then: It...was...on!"

"Thanks, dude." I said.

"You'd do the same for me."

"I would, and you know it." I stood up and held the notebook out, away from my chest. *Time to get rid of this thing. No sense holding onto something so awful. Wait, what?*

"Cole." I looked at him. His eyes reflected the fire. "You said Mani sensed me at Rick's place?"

"Yeah, I did," Mani answered, looking up at me. "It was faint, but I definitely sensed you. Why?"

I slowly backed away from the fire. *It can't be! No, it just...can't be?*

One by one, they each stood and moved toward me. I kept on stepping backward.

"Josh. What is it?" Emma pleaded.

"I…" I looked from Cole, to Mani, and finally to Emma. "I wasn't…ever at Rick's."

"I don't understand," Emma responded.

"What?" Mani nearly yelled. "But, that's not possible. I *know* I sensed you. I did."

"No," I leaned closer to her. "No, you didn't."

I turned quickly, running toward my truck. Each of them followed. Cole kept repeating, "What's going on? Where we going?"

On our way to Rick's, Mani explained it to Emma and Cole: "If he was never at Rick's, it wasn't Josh I sensed."

"Well, you were sick." Cole spoke with a quiver in his throat. "You made a mistake. Right?"

That's when the conversation in the truck ended. We found Rick's place empty, abandoned. No curtains, no furniture. The street lights cast weird shadows throughout the barren apartment. I walked around, looking in through each window. Nothing. *Where is he?* I turned, facing the apartment building's backyard. *The field! The hillside! The ledge, where we found Mani!*

So I took off in that direction, slowing down once I realized it was much darker back here, amongst the bushes and trees. I then turned and raised my hand, signaling the others to stay put. Cole lunged forward, though, only to be stopped by Mani's grasp. She shook her head. He wisely obeyed.

A twig cracked in the distance. The feeling was intense, too intense to just be Mani. A figure, dark and familiar, stepped out from behind a tree. Rick, yes, but this time dressed differently, with long, tighter-fitting jeans and a T-shirt, instead of the baggy shorts I'd seen him in before. His face: stern, rigid, sweaty.

Ready.

I moved toward him.

"I'd stay back, my friend."

"Why? You know about me: what I am, my strength. I'll kill you, friend."

"Yeah, I know *what* you are. And…you know what I am too, don't you?" He lifted his chin, glancing back at the others. "Mani knows, too, don't you sweetheart?" His smile: sick, taunting.

He said, "Why don't you fill the other two in?"

I didn't respond. *They need to leave. I have to keep them safe. But, can I even keep myself safe? I…feel… so…weak…again.*

"Fine. If you won't, I'll have to show them." Rick looked at the tree beside him, and with one swift blow of his arm, ***BAM***! Bark flew in all directions. The tree's foundation shook. We all (save for Rick) shielded our faces.

"What the hell?!" Cole screamed.

"Now that that's out of the way, we can get down to business. You see, *Josha*, it would benefit you greatly, to keep me happy. See?"

"Keep you happy?"

"If I'm happy, your little friends get to keep breathing." He leered at me. "And you and Mani get to stay here on your little dream planet. I'm sure you'd rather be here with your little girlfriend. Or would you prefer it if I send you both back…to Theos?" He gave a laugh.

I have no choice. He's stronger than me. I'll have to buy some time 'til I can find a way to take him down. "And what, exactly, will make you happy?"

"Why, it's simple." He walked past me, staring at the others, then back at me. "I want what you have. A new life on Earth. We are…partners…now."

"Partners? Never!"

"You might not like it, Josha, but it's the only way. And you know that." Before I could move, he grabbed both my arms and pinned them together behind my back. Burning sensations gripped me hard, from my shoulders down. *He'd rip my arms off if he wanted to. There's a reason he's keeping me alive.*

When Emma screamed out, he let go. I reached around awkwardly to rub the backs of my shoulders, and stood upright, trying to regain some dignity.

"You had to kidnap me and lock me in a cellar to get my attention?"

"Just knocking on your door for a little talk… wouldn't have been nearly as fun." He sneered.

I stepped over, filling the space between him and Emma.

"So, how does this…*partner thing*, work?"

"Josh, no," Mani yelled.

"We don't have much choice, Mani."

More teeth exposed by his newest smile. "We'll talk more later." He lunged at me. I jumped, raising my fists. He laughed out loud. "I'll be in touch."

His smile deflated as he raised his fingers to his temples, breathed in and out, and...vanished.

Emma ran to my side. Grabbing my arm, she asked, "He's...Theosian?"

I wrapped my arms around her, caressing her face, wiping away her tears.

"He can mask his presence if he doesn't want us to sense him," Mani said. "He can hide amongst us, any time he wants."

So they've followed us now. And he wants us alive, for some reason.

I have people I love to protect, now.

I don't know how, but I have to.

*He's strong, but I'll be stronger soon. And I'm smart, very smart. I have to figure out a way...*I held Emma close. I looked at Mani. And then the three of us, in sync with one another, looked at Cole.

THE END

CPSIA information can be obtained
at www.ICGtesting.com
Printed in the USA
FFHW01n0832230618
47181437-49865FF